SAM NORTH

Sam North has worked as an actor in the London fringe theatre and in a number of films. THE AUTO-MATIC MAN, which won the Somerset Maugham Award in 1990, is his first novel. He lives in London.

Sam North

THE AUTOMATIC MAN

Copyright © 1989 by Sam North

First published in Great Britain in 1989 by Martin Secker & Warburg Ltd.

Sceptre edition 1990

Sceptre is an imprint of Hodder and Stoughton Paperbacks, a division of Hodder and Stoughton Ltd.

Printed and bound in Great Britain for Hodder and Stoughton Paperbacks, a division of Hodder and Stoughton Ltd., Mill Road, Dunton Green, Sevenoaks, Kent TN13 2YA. (Editorial Office: 47 Bedford Square, London WC1B 3DP) by Cox and Wyman Ltd., Reading, Berks.

British Library C.I.P.

North, Sam
    The automatic man.
    I. Title
    823'.914 [F]

    ISBN 0-340-52904-0

One

I've been searching for a face. Everyone passing by me gets a good scrutiny now. D'you ever try and turn your own eyeballs into magnets, in the hope of catching something? Don't do it. I caught sight of myself in the Tesco window and I looked merely desperate, if not repellent. But over and over I have failed to recognise that person, or trap them, or win them. I do such things because I have been indulging too long in private. And why's all this privacy happened in the first place? Because I have had to come to terms with the surprise of finding myself in a predicament.

There are breaks in the time that we get to run along our own lifespan, when we fiddle messily with a bit of toast, and don't give a damn about the plate or the knife or the jam sticking to the table. That's where I am now; most of my hours seem to pass me by. I'm in a place where you find out that jam is sticky, and other unpleasant truths. I can be pressed up close enough to someone to see the grain in their skin and still comes the mournful thought that they're a different species. I've been so worked over by the Original Incident that everyone seems impossibly far away. I want my head held. I want someone who knows exactly how to do it, tight, with their open hands moving over the surface of my hot brain, and I will relax, breath by breath, and hide my face in the soft

1

corner of their neck, while they continue to press and stroke my brow.

My fingers are still cold from my latest dawdle on the balcony. That little jutting slab of concrete is the coldest place in the world.

It is unconscionable to think that while I'm waiting this person exists. She (it will be a female) is now walking around, unknowing, carried along until the umpteen millionth intersection of Time and Space brings us together. I need her now. I can't wait. If only I could tweak fate, or reach into her head and guide us into a start.

To set it up from this anonymous distance, I would begin by planting an episode into her head. It's not that I want to hurt her, I just want to share my own hurt. I'd want her to take some of it off me; she'd do it just by understanding.

It would be like hanging a picture in her head; the scene is this room with me as the sole occupant. I'd take her up close so she'd know me again. Then I'd fill the dark inside of her mind with this episode, putting her through it to make it stick. Her first task is to get me out of the front door. She'd have to take me by the scruff of the neck, using both hands, and march me into the corridor. She'd have to be firm. She might need to shout: 'Shut up! No complaints! Just do what I say!' She'd be standing there with her hands hurting my neck. I would describe to her how she'd be looking down a corridor, my corridor. It's gloomy, but at the end of the corridor there is one pin-prick of light. A spyhole. I'd have her shake me a little, like a bad dog, and instruct me, 'Look again at the spyhole. Look at it properly!' We'd walk down the corridor and she'd press her eye to the cold surface. We all know those wide-angle scenes.

It's all curled up to fit in the circle of your view. I'd ask her to swear that there's nothing there. So she'd tell me, 'See, there's no one there!'

I'd slip the locks on her memory, and continue inserting this important incident. On we'd go, opening the front door by turning the Chubb key, and then the Yale. Both locks are brand new. She'd have to learn to notice these things, to feel the quality of the mechanisms. My locks move smoothly. Solid, and sounding like they're dumb. They don't know any of my secrets, but they have a duty to safeguard them. Then I'll need to be given a shove to get me through the door.

I like talking to her. Wherever she is she won't know that I'm there, hanging loops of words in her head, but I persist.

'Outside you are suddenly in no man's land. These shared concrete stairwells are used to funnel the mass of the public to their front doors. There are hundreds of them. We will be passing a few. Old men patiently fit new locks, top, bottom, and middle. There's a rubbish chute on the first landing. Even the trash gets executed. We're walking past. These stairs go on . . . count ten flights . . .'

I'm sorry for what I am about to do, but I'll go through with it, in order that we might meet on a sound footing.

'Now we're outside and walking, it's not going to take too long. Friends?'

The sky opens when you walk out of the block. No more just the colour of the window, it's the real thing, like on my balcony. All the other blocks are there as usual, defying the sky. Hundreds of flats are arranged in the cheapest way possible. It's all been worked out on paper. This means that each flat is the same. Us people trot along the same dotted lines. The compartments in our minds are designed to shrink, in

3

order to cope somehow. Outside the front gates of the housing estate we would turn left and walk alongside the railings. Up to our left, the balcony with the fifteen small-size empty flower pots tied to the outside of the rail, that's my flat. That's where we started.

Now, it would be important, for the sake of this experiment, that she is feeling good. The last thing I ought to do is *scare* her. So I would fit the scene up appropriately, give her the sense that my hand is round her shoulder, say, tell her a really good joke. I'd arrange things well: there'd be money in her pocket, which she just got paid. It would have been a good week, whatever sort of week she'd like best. She'd have had a laugh, or worked and pushed herself bloody hard, or perhaps the sex is at the party waiting for her. The lines in the pavement pass beneath our feet. 'What I love,' I'd say, 'is the way you can ride the bounce of a new pair of trainers.'

The polished patent leather fashion boots are shining up at her. The Doc Marten's have just got run in. Whatever. There's hours of new time ahead of her, for her own use.

We turn round the corner and head for the Alley. It's a useful short cut, a tunnel under the railway line that only us local residents know about. The thunder of the train shakes the damp, old, forgotten brickwork, and we feel in the thick of it, nippy round the houses, saving ourselves some spare minutes with our knowledge of the city. We feel clever, and fit and well, and calm and peaceful, also, uncluttered with everyday worry, and adventurous, or we're fizzing with energy. We feel brave, as a matter of course. If there's anything we don't want, it doesn't matter. We can take our pick. We feel like the sort of people we ought to be.

We'd stop here in the Alley. I'd take her to the exact spot,

4

over by the soaking wall, where the sediments have crept together to make a thin bed of slime over the lumpy tarmac. Let the thunder from the train turn us forward a few hours; suppose that it's drawing a load of time over the top of us. It's brought us to a moment of crisis . . . She can remember the party. She has started the walk home . . . I would speak slowly inside her head:

'Now it's dark and you're out of breath from running. You've been running so hard, pounding the pavements, your arms pumping the air, useless limbs! You haven't bothered to check the roads for traffic, just run with instinct in your heels and fear threatening to catch at your neck; you're willing yourself to get home. Here in the Alley, they've caught you and held you. In this exact spot they stand leaning round you. All draw breath. One coughs on the outward gasps. Or is it a breathless laugh? One arrives late and bends over his knees to pump air. When they push you to the ground you feel the cool slip of the sediment on your cheek. Do you know the hand groping the back of your head? What's the connection? Why are they doing this to you? The hand presses your face into the slime, until the corner of your mouth hits the tarmac underneath. Your lip is pinched between your teeth and the ground. You gnash the mud to try for a chance at some air. Now is the time to tell you, now that you're struggling to pull your lip free, and they're pressing harder, and your bare tooth, you know, the sharp incisor at the corner, is being driven into the ground, now is the time for you to know that they are doing this for a fucking good reason. The best reason! Oh yes! They're doing this because they want to. You have been trying to take the strain onto your chin but the weight of the man, as he rocks back and forth with his hands on your head, over-

5

comes that effort at resistance. Your tooth is the victim. I haven't got good teeth. That one was capped, so it was already vulnerable. It snapped quite easily at the time, and the one next to it went too. How long would it take before yours would break? Anyway, now, for my sake, I want you to feel it levered against the gum, and then snap. They already had your money, back at the Original Incident. They already had your blood. Not serious blood, but now they find it again, and kick it, where it bleeds into your shirt. They kick it again. It's fun! They kick and they kick their own stab wound until it's got too long since you drew a breath and you lose consciousness. So you find the famous dumb blissful release at last, lying folded round the force of the incoming trainers.'

I would listen carefully when I finished, to see if there were any repercussions to my story. What shape does the inside of someone's character take? Will I recognise it from the outside?

You know the curious thing I remember after I lost consciousness? 'Thud.' It was nothing else. There was no more breathing, no more noises in their throats, no feeling of hands-on violence. I had no knowledge in me, no consciousness of them or of myself. But I do remember these rootless, vague 'thuds' drifting into my stomach. I didn't feel them. It was like a spiritual thing. I heard them with my inner ear. There. That's where I'm really fucking inescapably bruised; there, where no blood gets to, where there's no immunity, where no polypeptide chains can be called up to carry away the infection.

I don't think that I'm cruel myself. I have a motive: I want someone to be here with me in this hole that I've drilled myself into. I need someone to walk beside me, round and round in small circles in a bare flat in London. But I'm being selfish, forcing myself on her now and not waiting for her to intersect with me.

I'd pick her up and lift her arm round my shoulder. We hobble well together, don't we? Like in a war movie, if there was a bit of smoke. I'd take her home and wait to share her understanding.

She could say that she'd seen much worse; suffered trauma that's more concentrated and poisonous than what we've just gone through together. I considered that before I started, and decided that it didn't matter. We're not trying to put a premium on a particular sort of violence here. I don't care. Whatever it is that's blighted anyone's life in that way, it has an effect on me now. This is what happens: it makes me go sour with grief. I'm with them. I'm on their side, and I'm so fucking angry. It's the same when I watch any TV footage of the Nazi holocaust. I break into a shaking, blinding, automatic rage of sympathy. And I feel dirty and violent and burnt up with a thousand detailed considerations of my revenge, our revenge.

I tell you it's not television anymore. We've been forced to take it personally, she and I, as we make our way back to the safety of the flat. You know what the difference is? It's something frightening that's left behind when the bewilderment, the anger, the growling plans for revenge and the utterances on justice have all been worked out and cast aside. It's the answer. It's what it all boils down to. It is *fear* that makes all the difference.

'We're passing by the railings now, struggling along under each other's arm. Not far to go. Your eyes are unwilling to look very much around you. I would guess that they feel dull. However, I promise you that they are working better than ever before. They only look glazed and shuttered because they are seeing too much of a bad thing. These railings? No, not railings, not simple railings put up to stop people getting in. Not for you. It's no wonder your eyes are closing, because now the railings show themselves to you, they talk to you, they say, "Here we are, a row of rusty spears welded together and set in concrete. We are waiting for the next accident! We are waiting for the next suicide . . ."'

In the flats directly above, each inhabitant has a private door onto a small concrete balcony.

Climbing the stairwell I'd have her look down at our feet, trying to control the difficult operation of getting hers moving one after the other up the steps, past the little individual tragedies of the cigarette ends, smeared flat into the concrete, the stained filters levered up, in pain. The door is ours; the keys fit. The locks obey. It's a pleasure, how smoothly they move. They slide behind us, sealing out the danger.

I admit to the charade. We know what we're talking about now. One isolated human, bitten by fear, infected by fear, inventing a friend like a school kid . . .

There's one more thing. I'd leave it until a bit later to say it to her. Perhaps I'd visit again when she sleeps. I'd whisper, 'Go and look through the spyhole again. It's not the same, is it? You approach it now with a certain reverence. The distortion is alarming. You see him now? That tall figure is waiting for us day and night. He lives there, on the landing outside the front door. See the cloak draped over his arm? He will hold that out for us, and every time we step past him we have to take the weight of it, even though it reeks of fear. He will have a very courteous expression on his face. He is never anything but graceful and polite in his behaviour towards us, but this makes us hate him all the more, because obviously this facetiousness indicates the pleasure he takes in his cruel duties.

His slow-moving gestures and his pretence at giving "advice" ... He is persistent, assiduous, loathsome. He is called the Opponent. See, you are not finding it easy to open the door and walk over the threshold, because of what he makes you feel.'

The flat is empty. It's barely got any furniture in it. It is not a home until 'she' arrives. This isn't good enough, how it is now, me filling in my time with inventions. I shall increase my searching in the streets for a face. I need to magnetise my glare to everyone because it'll attract the effort of her touch. It isn't possible, is it, for an invention to take me into the bedroom, lay me down, hold my head tightly in its hands, and press the surface of my brow with its thumbs?

Move them in patterns. Repeat them over and over, until they're something I can be sure of; then I can go to sleep.

No, I'm asking too much. This is something that's not allowed. I make my heart slow down by commanding the blood-throbs to drop from around my ears back down to my chest, while I laughingly repeat to myself a list of my favourite things. How much longer am I going to have to wait?

November 3

I am in danger of losing my job. Several times this week I've turned up late. The manager has simply looked at me with a measure of curiosity. He wants me to explain, to tell him that it's all a mistake, that he's not going to lose his chef. My speciality is a blackcurrant steak, and he doesn't want to lose the blackcurrant steak because it brings in folding cash. The

9

blackcurrant steak . . . it's ridiculous to cry over such an absurd thing. The waitress Sally heard me in the staff bog and came in. I'd been waiting for somebody, anybody, so I'd left the door unlocked. She asks the question in a voice for babies, dropping on one knee in front of my throne of unhappiness:

'What is it?'

' . . . the blackcurrant steak! Bloody thing!'

'What about it?'

'I can't do it any more. I can't. I'm sorry.'

'You do it fine . . . you're the only one who can do it.'

'That's . . . that's the bloody trouble. Why can't someone else do it for once?'

'I know, I know. I'm fed up with this place too.'

She speaks kindly. She is putting some real effort into me. There's a genuine search of my face going on. So why can't I use her? Because she hasn't got the face. She's like a professional. I couldn't take someone who so obviously looks like they want to help *me*. That would be too humiliating. I take the knife from where I had stuck it into the loo paper, and hold it down the length of my knee.

'Look at this thing,' I say. 'What is this thing?'

'I think we ought to get back to work now.' She's put on a firm voice. She wants to control the knife, it's frightening her.

'It's a . . . It's a *knife* . . . ' I gasp over the last word. My tears are dried up. It feels like my eyes are smoking. 'Have you any idea,' I continue, 'how difficult it is to say that word?'

'What is the matter? What are you crying about? I can't help until I know.'

'That's the worst . . . that's what's so fucking stupid . . . it's nothing. There's no reason!'

I start to laugh. The laughter dissolves our worry like magic,

10

and she joins in happily. The trouble in the bog with the chef is all part and parcel of the soap opera of the restaurant. It's all television. Sally leaves, still laughing. I dangle the . . . thing, the thing with the blade and the handle . . . I put the tip of the blade to my scar and suddenly, like it was red hot, I drop the knife in a thrill of horror at imagining myself gutless.

My search for the face goes on. The restaurant is a good place. I have a licence to observe the faces. When I see her I shall make a special Chef's Trip out amongst the tables to enquire whether the food is satisfactory. I shall arrive at her side and ask her several solicitous questions. She won't be eating the blackcurrant steak, and when I ask her why not, she will say she is a vegetarian. I will then describe how the quarter-carcasses arrive in a recognisable shape, and how I have to take my own set of . . . my half-dozen . . . – they can only be described as my personal set of *weapons* – to deal with the animal, and there and then, in the middle of my quiet bloodthirsty description, I shall throw down my apron at her feet and say, 'Never again.'

The little girl in the park came up to me because I was talking to her dog. She was friendly and confident and we sat down eventually because we were talking for such a long time. I became interested when she said she didn't like boys. When I asked her why not she said she didn't know. I pressed her.

'Why, what is it about boys?'
'Something.'
'There's something about boys?'
'Yes. Something that puts you off.'
'Is it something cruel?'
'Yes.'

11

'Are you afraid of boys?'

'Yes.'

I felt moved with pity and friendship. Here in this miniature person was a smaller version, an understanding, but with lower horizons, of everything that is threatening to drown me out of my own life. It was when I looked over at her and saw how her fine hair blew across her face, and how her clumsy half-made hand drew it back, and how her eyes glistened newly-made, her smile holding steadily and eagerly in spite of her fear of boys; that's when I nearly made a fool of myself. I considered telling her the details of my own fear, how I was not 'afraid of boys' but afraid of one particular sort of boy, someone who'd bashed me up in the playground, but that yes, she was right, every boy had that mean streak in the colour of his eye that could turn him into a mad dog. What stopped me from saying all this was that I remembered: I am a boy.

November 7

There he is, the gloomy slow-moving figure, every time I open the front door. The Opponent has his own history that I'll tell you about one day. He holds the cloak out, performing his grim little duty with the sick, minimal sort of pleasure that he's only just capable of. I have to step into the cloak, despite the death-smell of fear, and I have to carry it on my shoulders all the time I am out. It drags me down, so heavy with butterflies that I feel immobilised by the weight of it. I creep like a leaden crow, with my head down to avoid looking at anyone.

An ambulance gave me an idea. I pray fervently every time an ambulance goes past now. Sometimes you can see shady figures through the darkened windows, and I address them directly and extravagantly: 'Good luck! Whatever happened, all the luck that there is, all the good luck that I can drag out of this fucking city, have it! Have it all!' Even if one of the most heinous criminals has just been scraped off the tarmac and put in the back there, I think it's a place which could change him, because he would be suffering. I could watch him suffering.

This ambulance set me thinking of the war and the past generation of people who signed on the dotted line and found themselves having horror for breakfast, lunch and tea every day for five years. Some people, I had heard, who had no physical courage, could suddenly find it in them if they became ambulance drivers. It's because they were free from the aggression of it all; they were released from the posturing. They enjoyed a different sort of courage. Maybe I could find something for myself in their mould.

So it was on my day off that I did something about it.

I've managed to get out of the door past the Opponent. Fuck him and his evil-smelling blanket that he holds out for me. I can still hold up under his garment. I'm starting out on my way to the ambulance station to see about getting a new chance. I dread this first corner, because I have to volunteer to walk towards the Alley. (The usual order to myself: cross the road. Always walk past it on the other side.) As I round the corner my sight fidgets all over the rubbish at the entrance, looking for dead bodies and discarded babies, and I probe deep in the perspective of it, planning revenges. I hate it. It's like how my fingers work on a spot on my back. You wish the thing would disappear, but you can't help touching it, making it worse.

As I shift myself round the shoulder of the corner I remember (again) hearing that scream from the building on my right. It was a short scream, forced out with a garbled intensity that could never break glass. I stopped at the time, and looked up. There was still evidence of an old sign nailed to the wall: ' . . . Council . . . development of 64 Maisonettes . . .' From behind the sign came the girl's cry again. It was breathless and clumsy. It was a terrified noise coming from a strange throat as I stood hopeless and powerless. There were other sounds, like she was being assaulted. Every few seconds I heard more of the muffled shouts and screams coming out of the maisonette. You will understand what mental paralysis this put me into. I knew that I was going to turn on my heel and walk down the road. It's not that I ignored the cries. I already know I shall remember them for ever. Now I have to retrace the route every day, and I look up at the silent row of windows, waiting for a sign, or evidence, or some form of relief. As I walked away that time I felt that each step was responsible for another injury to her, and I remember those energetically recoiling steps each time I mark them again. I am disgusted at the sickness that's infected me so thoroughly.

I pass through the market on my way to the ambulance depot, and as usual cast an eye over the jewellery stall to check for anything that might have turned up. It's not very likely to appear here, but I'm curious.

If I had been an ambulance driver, would I have gone into that screaming house? What d'you think, would a polyester uniform and a funny hat have made any difference? I can imagine that there would be something there that would have helped me deal with my fear. I would have had a role to hold onto – something to do with the vehicle, and the uniform, and the other people with me, all in the same uniform, all expecting each other to go in. I would have been carried by the momentum. It would be my job, my paid work, to go in.

Always the girl's screams will run and run and run.

At the ambulance station a man treats my enquiry with quiet good humour. 'Don't want to work here, surely not?' he says, and takes me over to another man in an office, who's wearing a different uniform. I repeat my question to him. He replies:

'Recruitment is all done centrally now. I'll give you the address to write to for an application form. But I can tell you that you do about two or three years driving the old people about before they let you do the stuff you see on television. Only a small percentage make it. The right people.'

I take the form and say thank you, and leave the yard. The men and women that I had seen in the office and around the vehicles had something going here. They made an atmosphere, which I had briefly stepped into. I wanted to stay, to share a quiet joke with the first man, to follow an order, simply and correctly, from the second man, to be part of things.

As I sit here looking out of the window I wonder what I'm doing. Would you believe that in the beginning I thought the whole thing would disappear after a few aspirins and a talk with some policemen? Since then I have shrugged and struggled and delayed. Now I'm going to open the whole thing up and I don't care if it turns out to be a can of worms.

I keep on returning to the screams that sent me spurting down the road that time with my own inward cries. Right here from this window I can see the corner and the row of flats that the council calls 'maisonettes'. They run along the opposite side of the road to my block, only three storeys high to our

15

twelve storeys. I can see the three square windows. What happened? I checked the local paper to see if there was any news. Sometimes I indulge myself with a private anger when I read those little violent paragraphs in the local paper. 'An eighty-seven-year-old crippled widow is recovering in hospital after three masked men ... ' And so I might rage, frustrated, full of energy that's powerless, that has no root, because of fear.

November 10

In the dark I listen to the noises within this giant block of patterned concrete. Some of them are familiar: an inexplicable rattle from upstairs, a sporadic row in a foreign language barely muffled by my bedroom wall. Yes, I agree, I need to hang on to something; I need a peg, set somewhere in the future, to reach out for, to stop all this darkness from crowding me in. The face that I'm looking for has been born, has grown up, is walking around somewhere, perhaps not very far away. She just needs to come close enough for me to recognise her. What can you do about fate? How can you hustle a chance along faster?

I'm not looking for sex, or prettiness. I like the way a woman's body works, and the practice of getting a good fit between the male and female skin, and the progress of a smile, and a sexual stance to the eye, but I've seen all this and it's not what I want. The face, when I find it, will speak to me. It will be something to do with kindness.

I'm thinking of placing an advert. It is humiliating to answer one, but it can't be much else other than interesting to put one in.

There was a time this week when I poured alcohol down my throat until it sang in my blood. I was at work, and I took exception to the apron of the sous-chef.

'We are here,' I say grimly, 'to give a show to them out there.' I wave at the dining-room, which could be seen through a hatch in this part of the kitchen. 'Please do not come in here with blood smeared . . . all over your apron.'

'I have to carry the meat . . .' he complains.

'No butchering! No butchering in here. Take these!' I hand him the block of wood holding my own collection of Victorinox knives. 'Take this!' I say, and hand him the cleaver from its hook. 'Go and butcher out there. Come back to me only with steaks laid out on a platter. This is a showcase, not a bloodbath.'

He is surprised at the change in rules. These things that I am heaping into his arms were previously sacred, for my use only. I am glad to see the back of them, and feel happy enough to make up a brand new verse for the Hissing Song. I catch a glance from a porter, busy in the outer kitchen, but I am safe here in my grotto, with my silly hat, on display for the public. When that sort of money has to be eased out onto the side-plate, they need to know that the whole restaurant is not run by a gang of students with a freezer and a microwave.

I don't mind that my future lies in de-stalking blackcurrants, for now. I don't think I will lose my job for singing the Hissing Song. I think I have more of a problem: I want to lose my job, because work means having to get home. At the weekends I am safe, because we stay busy until late, so I get given a taxi. In the week, if we close up before midnight, then I have to go on public transport. This journey is my sticking point. Every night of it is routine hell. I feel so sick, setting out, that I could

17

justify calling for an ambulance to get me home. Sirens full blast.

November 20

There have been developments from the Screaming Maisonette. I was walking past with the rain bouncing around my feet, and I saw a woman sitting on the steps, fed up with making an effort to shrink herself into the partial shelter. There were several clues – she had a collection of cases with her, she had no coat or umbrella, and she was sitting on the stairs that lead up to the Screaming Maisonette. When I got home, from my viewpoint on the fifth floor, I could still see her in the left-hand corner of my front window. Whatever happened to her in the confines of the maisonette, the rest of the world turned deaf, and I was the one who hurried away, deafest of all. Now what? She'd been driven out? Were we all going to maintain the city tradition and go blind until she disappeared of her own accord? That argument I heard, about how making no choice is a choice in itself, that applied here. As I sat doing nothing, watching the figure blurred by the rain on my window, I might as well have been turning a hose on her myself.

November 22

I have just seen a film. It was a documentary about Tibet, and followed a certain ritual that takes place as part of the religious scene up in the mountains. The men prepared themselves for this one day which was spent in the temple on the mountainside. Some rocked back and forth and knocked out single beats from the skin drums with a curved stick. Some chanted. There was incense, sent out in spinning puffs of smoke by the man swinging the container. It all amounted to a tiny collection of devout people, descended from a consistent history, gathered on the side of a mountain so vast it could have been one of the haunches of this planet; and the pin-point, the focus of the whole ceremony, was a single man dancing with a short curved dagger. His dance was slow; one step could take minutes to move to its conclusion. The dagger led the dance; the man, its partner, followed in a tortuous pattern. The idea was that the man would engage with the dagger, and if it all went right, the dagger would enter him and cut out all the bad feeling that had built up in him throughout the year. He would be exorcised.

There are lots of reasons why it doesn't work with me in my small square room. I am in amongst a whole messy pile of other human beings, millions of them, and a dagger is a kitchen tool or a weapon for snatching things with, and it is impossible to stitch together even a few minutes of concentration. When I bring the kitchen implement towards me in a repeat of one of his moves, I feel an increase in the volume of my bad feeling. I have a bad feeling about the dagger itself. I have not got the ability to impart any symbolic power to the knife; the brutal facticity of it holds me bewitched. It's like the cold dullness of a shark's eye. It has literally got under my skin. Even if I went to Tibet tomorrow I couldn't pick up a foreign belief and put it on like a coat. I can never have another history, I'm landed here dealing with this.

19

I have every reason to be proud. At this very minute she is in the spare room! I have been busy, trotting round to buy a second-hand bed and a dressing table from the Oxfam furniture store. As I write this she is laying her stuff out, a stranger in a new place. Tomorrow I will put up a hanging rail. We have agreed on a minimal rent for such a small room in a flat that is virtually empty of any furniture.

I am still not sure about her face. She is older than me, but even taking that into account her face is harsh. It is one of those faces . . . it looks like you could go splitting logs with it. (She is not trying to be quiet in there. I can hear her cough, and the drawers tunnelling in the dresser.) It's not that her face is battered, it's just that she looks sharp. Why do I feel servile when I talk to her? I don't think she will be very tolerant of anything I might give away about myself. She has a prickly, not very sympathetic heat in her eye.

Not only that; there is more excitement. The advert is in. Mine is in the style of those ones that are brutally self-recriminatory with the intention of being impressively funny. I bought a box format and made a go of it:

> Isolated, fearful, hangdog chef, lost in
> maze of concrete, seeks a female face with
> a light like Florence Nightingale's. I'll
> lick your wound if you'll lick mine.

It looks ridiculous. I can imagine people all over the city sneering at the ad. They'll read through them all, same as I do, scanning quickly to find sex and distress. This week's list. But somewhere, my face, the one that I'm waiting for, will read, and feel her interest quicken.

December 3

Her name is Chrissy, my tenant, who wears the short skirts. She works in quality control for a food manufacturer. That makes her a technician, or a scientist, I suppose. I didn't ask for details. She thought I would want to have a reference from her employer. That's the last thing I should be worried about, when you consider just what I had to do to get her in here. I had to find the end of a long length of effort to get to the point of having enough courage to help her. Bugger the references! Still, I find I have an immediate reward. There is a great wash of confidence, a new weapon for my personal security; I feel as safe as a new lock, all because there's another person in the flat. Now that I've done my bit and got her out of trouble I can give myself an easier ride for whatever happened in the Screaming Maisonette, even if what I did at the time wasn't exactly television.

Nothing has changed, however, beyond the spyhole, outside the sanctuary of these dotted lines that mark my particular flat. The Opponent lounges, with the mantle draped over his arm, waiting. He is not disconcerted by Chrissy moving in. I creep out onto the landing, and he asks me, as he holds out the cloak, 'Is this trip necessary?' Just with one look, he says that. While he fastens the single crimson button, he doesn't waste time. He's relentless in his suave cynicism: 'If you're going to work, it's to go and handle dead flesh. And then think of it; you find yourself at the end with the walk home. That bastard dark creepy violence!' he says, and continues with his sideways eyes, 'When you are trying to escape from it, it follows you, and keeps on reminding everyone that yes, it's you, you ... it's pointing at you; you're the butt, burning yourself up with it, turned over by it, your mind's tipped; you're skewered at the end of a great mass of fear, you're so fucked you see nothing around you, no sky, no buildings, no people that haven't been corrupted by the invasion of criminal intent!' Even as I shoulder the weight of the cloak, and start the descent to ground level, he goes on, calling after me something theatrical, like, 'Going down to the shops? Why? You'll only be reminded of the filth caught by the gaps in between paving stones! Why bother with the shops, when you have to carry the cloak?' And then you get his horrible tight laugh. It's not a comfortable sound in his throat.

Unfortunately we work at different times, Chrissy and I, but still, sometimes, at weekends or what not, I will be able to walk out of the door following her fashionable, bulky coat. That is some relief, to trot like a dog hiding behind her heels! She won't know.

She's still keeping to herself behind the spare room door. As I have been moving back and forth with tea and a plate of Spinach Daisy, she has been listening to music, and now everything's gone quiet. Perhaps she's decided to sleep. Her presence in this flat has given some potential to these rooms. I wish I could interpret tea-leaves, or read some pattern in the dried shards of spinach on my plate. There is a crowded atmosphere here, and one of those silences just filled enough with distant noises to make it pregnant. As I walk past her closed door it strikes me that the room is loaded.

Chrissy says, 'There were two calls. One from Rachel, again
. . . and the other, from Elaine . . . Elaine Partridge. She asked
you to call her back, and left a telephone number.'

'Ah yes . . . Elaine.' I speak as though I know the girl, to
cover for the fact that I am pursued by embarrassment. 'Oh
God,' I reply briskly, 'I can't be bothered.' I hope Chrissy
doesn't guess what the struggle is. We are still noticing more
than we speak out loud. We're fidgeting, trying to outdo each
other in the presentation of our helpful habits. This has been a
typical example of our conversation this last week, occurring
in the late afternoon when Chrissy comes home from work,
before I've left for the restaurant. We give the telephone
messages then, sharing them in conscientious detail; not like
good friends. Rachel? Elaine? Who are these people? The truth
is that I've made a blunder with the amount of girls I replied
to. Replying to any was a mistake. Advertising was a mistake.
You can't force fate. You can bully away, and it always appears that you're right at the edge of fate's influence, but then
suddenly it proves itself, revealing itself to you again as a
further horizon, bigger and cleverer than you think. It turns
out that you've not been forging a path for yourself; instead
you've been had, tricked into stumbling across an even larger
desert. Look how things always, at the last minute, *twist*, to
make you sense that breathtaking conception that you are
pitted against something that's beyond your puny fiddling
efforts. My idea of adverts was necessary, because it had to be
taken and used for something else. I'm like the insect that you
discover behind the wardrobe: you play with it; you watch it
struggling over the terrain with all its legs in drive, you put a

finger down in front of it, and it turns in a new direction, and ploughs ahead, unknowing, blind and out of breath. When I couldn't dredge up one single moment of courage to enable me to go and speak to the girl on the step, I put down my idea for her rescue on paper; and I failed to hand that over to her according to plan. When I saw her again I was so close I could have touched her; I could have put my finger down in front of Chrissy, and trapped her here in my flat. But still the moment of action got stuck, frustratingly ambushed somewhere along the chain of command. Then I had a use for the idea of the advert. Some of my cards are still in the shops, stuck with Blu-tack next to grotty ads for handymen and prostitutes.

But the girls from the mag – I don't know why, I don't want them any more. I've not made a single appointment since writing the replies. Each time Chrissy gives me a message from one of my invisible intangible potential succorers I re-member the photos in my drawer, a whole pack of faces: which one was Elaine? Who cares? They all looked stupid; they couldn't avoid it, because they (stupidly) replied to a ghoulish and sentimental advert. And now these names, with their faces stacked in my box, are cropping up every day, trying to get at me. Some of them have rung three or four times.

I think it's because Chrissy is here now, and it's nearly always been her who takes the calls and formally gives me the message. It makes me feel furtive. Her gaze is always so steady, that I'm sure it must be because she's restraining her curiosity. My secrecy has been spoiled. I am retreating, avoid-ing sideways in a quicksand of lies, like a crab, in order to reform my strategy against the Opponent in a way that won't expose me to Chrissy's judgement. Her judgement could be a very cold wind, if I was caught out and about without my shell. As for now, it's working between us. I saw a smile settle on her for a moment, when I shrugged off Elaine and Rachel. I had to load up my voice with a mysterious, disaffected tone: 'Ah . . . Elaine,' and it cheered her enough for the smile. Both of us lifted a bit.

There has been very little talk between us about our previous lives. I hardly ever begin one considered sentence without intending it to lead me into being able to ask her about the Screaming Maisonette. I can never quite get to the topic because it makes me feel the same as when I have to ask someone for money. I think that we are both valuing our privacy. It's a mounting pile between us. It could be an enjoyable store of discoveries.

She had no mark on her face, not even when she first came, but she might have got hit on the body. After all, my own wound lies hidden; it's a rind of hairless skin where the body has welded itself miraculously.

It would be something I could usefully do as a last desperate mission before jumping off the balcony: I could stand with a clipboard, accosting passers-by, counting the wounds underneath people's shirts. If I had the courage.

At the moment she is beginning to expand outside the boundaries of her small room. At first it was only to give me the phone messages from people like Elaine. Now she sits on the kitchen stool when she gets in, and hangs her coat on the same nail on the back of the door. I felt absurdly proud and emotional when I saw her coat silently embracing mine, like in those TV documentaries when the hunted vixen, thin and starving, steps within range of the infra-red camera and takes the food that the researchers have put out. We no longer have

25

separate shelves in the fridge, or any sort of rota for cleaning up; it's becoming easy.

We have also made plans to get some bits and pieces, chairs and so forth. She is polite about the blankness of the flat, not commenting on my two pictures and the fat hard chair I sit in when I'm looking out of the window. She's never shown the slightest curiosity about my bedroom, and keeps her own bedroom door closed whether she's in there or not. I caught a glimpse once when she was coming out, of the end wall decorated with some sort of cloth pinned to it, and a tape-machine on the floor surrounded by wasted cassette covers. She doesn't press too hard, but suggestions float from her careful voice every now and again: a carpet in the hall, a few more chairs, comfy ones, maybe a suite, a bath mat. I always fall into line with her suggestions, after a polite display of questioning uncertainty. Once she brought back flowers and that made the place look sadder than ever.

January 5

The news is that the Opponent is winning. Not just because of his insinuated accusations and posturing. Of course, yes, I am staying in, by way of avoiding the fear-sickness of going out, but also because staying in has become more interesting.

Let's say that I'm looking in the bathroom mirror. I see a man aged twenty-two with sallow skin that hangs loosely round a collection of unremarkable features, framed by hair hanging in long curves. The topmost line of my eye turns down at the outer end, making me look like a starving dog before I even

26

start trying. My eyes are black, set quite close at the top of my nose, which curves in the Roman style. I am of medium height, and on the thin side. When I stand naked in front of the mirror, you can see a clear pattern of what's laid out underneath my skin. Hair runs the usual course up my middle, spreading to a sparse fan on my chest. In that Shortest Possible Glance that you would give me if you passed by in the street, you might say, 'Frenchman' or 'Bistro chef'.

The bathroom mirror is a new way of passing time for me. It's not unpleasant, but I did without it before Chrissy produced it from one of her Saturday afternoon boxes. The medicine cabinet behind it is stuffed with soaps and sprays – all presents that Chrissy keeps. She uses them one by one. My blue hippo sponge is no longer alone on the side of the bath. He is almost obscured by dried plants and sea shells. It is like lowering yourself into a theme park, now, getting in the bath. Chrissy has had raging arguments with the man in the rent hatch about the damp on the walls in the bathroom. She hates the man in the rent hatch. He's glad of his reinforced hole to hide in.

When you leave the bathroom you step out into the corridor, which is wide enough for two people to pass except where the fusebox and gas meter are fixed into a white cupboard. The front door is right there on your left. It has a frosted glass panel in the middle of it with the spyhole on top. The front door is the gateway to the outside world. (The Opponent is becoming much more confrontational. He has taken to raising his hand as though he were a traffic policeman controlling my will-power. Sometimes I think he might speak; it would be a short dramatic phrase, uttered in sinister undertones. I would reply in the same style, something like 'Curse your uplifted hand!') The corridor has a carpet. You can walk down to the bedroom at the end without your feet touching the cold floor. This is all thanks to Chrissy, who brought it all back with her at various times, different Saturdays. As you walk down the corridor the kitchen is on the right next to the bathroom. It's a well-organised set-up with stainless steel surfaces made to my own specification. It's my job that made me fussy about it. Next to the kitchen is the spare bedroom. Chrissy's bedroom, I should say. Next to her, at the end of the flat, is my bedroom. Opposite from her, on the other side of the corridor, is the lounge. It's a room with a condensation problem. Pools of water leave tide-marks on the painted window-sill in winter. From this side of the block you get a wide view over the city of London. The window takes up most of one wall, spreading the city like a living map onto the mind of someone who spends too long in this room. The square mile of stomping-ground beneath the window is well pegged out in my mind with the place-names: the Screaming Maisonette; the place of the Original Incident; the Jewellery stall; the Tube; the Alley. At night the window turns into a flat display of lights shining through your own reflection in the glass.

Behind the wall is somebody else's lounge exactly the same but back to back. There live the people who have the rows, the fighting in a foreign language, that I can hear either when I'm lying in bed or in here looking out of the window. Terrible long sentences of gibberish in a deep voice from him are cut into by her sharp commands and her screams that aren't fearful screams, more like things designed to make him shut up. The pattern of the flat is repeated six hundred and twenty times in blocks on three sides. I bothered to count. We're on the fifth floor, with the standard broken steel box that used to be a lift.

I've travelled hours of time in front of the big window in the lounge, either standing with my elbows on the sill or sitting in the fat chair, focusing alternately on the outside world and then on my reflection. A fly on the window, crawling along up here on the fifth floor, would see me standing thinking, facing up to something that you can't organise out of your life, thinking thinking round and round the bloody little serpent, banging my head against nothing and it still hurts. I could open the door out onto the little balcony, and scramble over the rail untidily; it would be exciting to begin with and I'd be curious about the end. I could do it out of sheer curiosity, and to escape the utter misery of being this side of the fence. There's a carrot dangling in front of me and I'm being thrashed from behind. But I don't want to lose. I want to turn round and snap the bloody stick into little pieces. I refuse. I'll drag something out of the muddle and it'll be the answer.

My pictures are in the lounge. There are one or two more now belonging to Chrissy but they don't have the same effect, being photos of her family and a picture that her niece drew which says 'Krisy'. My two pictures hang one at each end. The one up near the door is by Salvador Dali, entitled *The Anthropomorphic Cabinet*. It shows a figure reclining on the floor, propped up on the full length of his arm, with a series of drawers coming out of his stomach and chest. A crumpled piece of cloth is hanging out of the third drawer. The topmost drawer comes out just underneath his chin, draped with hair that has run down from where it sprouts out of the middle of his face. The figure is painted with an intense lucidity. It looks so weird in detail that you can't believe it, but you recognise it.

29

He has one arm outstretched towards a distant doorway that lets out onto a street scene where ordinary people are walking about. I'm uncertain as to whether he's reaching out for help with that arm, or inviting people into his empty brown space, but whichever it is it makes him look ill and lonely. It's a poster from an exhibition that I found and pasted onto a board to make it look real. I cut all the printed words off and it hangs without a border or a frame.

At the other end of the room facing the Dali is a picture by a man called Chaissac. It is a face painted in a naive style and coloured green. The eyes are large and distinctly coloured. One is soft and kind to you when you look at it; the other, the violent yellow one, looks angry enough to kill you, and it would be for a good reason, because the rage, although painted in a shallow yellow, comes at you with persistent tenacity. Growing from the top of the head is a thick stem on top of which is set a curved growth. This growth is the answer to everything. If you were to look into the kind eye that responds to pity and ask the face, 'Why?', it would with a gentle lift of the eye indicate the growth as the reason. The growth, you see, has an absurd banana shape in it, as well as two patches of green reflected from the face. When you shift your gaze back onto the kind eye again, it's easy to understand its sadness. If you look into the angry eye, and ask, 'Why?', it would lift a finger and jab it into your own growth so hard it would make you wince. There's no escape from the growth. It has a depth to it, almost obscured by the cloudy mauve, but not quite. The depth is behind the picture. This Chaissac, fair enough, is only a print pasted onto a block again to try and make it look original, but it's hanging in the perfect place, better than an art gallery could do, because behind the wall is the next-door lounge. When I hear the rows coming through as a fast succession of his angry unintelligible sounds intersected with her short, commanding screams, I look at the Chaissac face and see the weight of the growth on the stem and the anger and the sadness and it all makes perfect sense.

I am here, doing nothing, using up my time. I'm under siege, and until I can find some weapons I can only order myself to retreat. I frequently telephone the restaurant saying that I'm ill, and then I can look forward to staying here in the evenings. They pretended sympathy at first, but now they are suspicious, and docking my pay every time. No doubt they are making plans to find a replacement before they sack me. Luckily I have some money, not much, but it would shelter my meagre appetites for some months. Even during the day I only go out if I really have to. Admittedly Chrissy has made it easier for me. My cash is disappearing at half the rate because she's here, and the place is more comfortable. There's a choice of three chairs to sit in and a table by the window with a plastic table-cloth on it and a sandwich toaster, but most of all, there is Chrissy herself. She has no idea what she means to me. I would never tell her that we have a history, a secret one-sided history that goes back before the first time we met. I promise, right now, that I will never ask her any questions. It's a difficult promise to make. Whenever she comes in I am always reminding myself of my initial cowardice with her screams galvanising me into nothing but wild thought, the imaginings of what I should have done, what I would have done, in there, facing him as he holds his hands in that position which is always hurting her. I notice that I have given

31

him the same identity as my own attacker at the Original Incident.

The thought that I had when she first came in, as I first saw her in the frame of the front door, was that she is a gift to me. Every time I hear her keys twisting back and forth to open the Chubb lock, and then again with the brand new little Yale, I think the same: 'She's a gift.' It's a responsibility.

Her face is still closed to me. There was once when she smiled and laughed at me, and suddenly it was as if blinds had been flung up from behind her eyes. Her look is sharp and harsh, as I said, but then it was playing against its type for a while. It was because of a joke surrounding all those calls I got from strange women; God knows how strange they must have been.

This ribbing she gave me over the phone calls marks the beginning of a step we're taking towards each other. Certainly I seized on it as a sign of offered friendship. The joke recurs with different lines from time to time and each run of exchanges is a confirmation of where we both want to go with each other. But, I admit, approaching this face of hers is going to be difficult. To lean towards it, however much I want to, might give me the sensation of an army deserter sidling up to the Sergeant-Major to sneak off with the water bottle.

I say this because of the story she told me about her fending off the muggers. She'd refused to let go of her bag and had fought and screamed until the strap broke. She'd relived her vindictive pleasure as she told me about her satisfaction at seeing one of the three, a girl, having to hitch herself along with a limp on the escape run.

However, one part of her face always fascinates me: her

mouth. She's got a mouth which is set crooked. The tilt of it makes it very watchable and appealing. Sometimes I have found myself being crude, watching her mouth for long periods of time when she's not aware of it. It's just a food-hole, but it always looks inclined towards elegance. I want to look after it. It closes clumsily but gracefully after any forkful of food or series of words. Set askew in that space between a pointed nose and a hard chin, it gives rise to an incredible feeling of fondness in me. It reminds me of a lame bird.

I have a new word, which is designed to help me avoid or hide the horribly formed person that I have become. The word is 'Item'. It comes from one particular project in my life when I was a kid. I'm using it as a collective noun, to cover those two sets of things that make my guts corkscrew more than any-thing else. So now, when I see a knife, any type of knife, I can say to myself, 'Item,' instead of 'Knife,' which is a word that always makes me start. 'Knife!' – it's as if the word itself creeps up to me, invisible in its own darkness, and runs into my ear. Similarly, that one type of male, the one who is responsible for the word 'male' being used as the start of the word 'malevo-lence', that one I recognise as an 'Item' also. The sight of him twinges on my spine, turning my look to the ground. At worst he is an extraordinarily specific idea, a model of the man in the Original Incident, even down to the sort of overcoat he was wearing.

This using of a private word is the beginning of my bid to treat the whole thing in a more scientific manner. I'm trying to pin it down, and give it some nomenclature. It's like calling the Black Death by another less emotional name, say,

'Bubonic Contagion'; you can then hold it off at the end of a stick and deal with it in a more rational manner. I'm looking for theories, with an answer at the end, allowing an escape. It must be possible. I wasn't like this before; it's something I've journeyed into. When I think of it as a journey, I can believe that I'm going to get out of it. It's like a hostile country that I've got lost in. When I think back, I nearly laugh: it's ludicrous, what sort of homegrown, untravelled simpleton I was; and I don't have to look that far behind me.

I'll go back ten months, for example. This would be not long before the Original Incident. I am lying asleep in my bed when I'm woken by a loud and repeated knocking at the door. The fist is banging against the glass panel. It's three in the morning, I see by the diodes next to my bed. I get up and find the underpants and walk down the corridor. I can see the shadows of two men moving blurred in the glass panel of the door. I don't bother with the spyhole. I undo the rattling little Yale lock and pull the door open. Two policemen ask me if I am Mr George Emery. I reply 'No,' and they apologise for disturbing my sleep, turning away to start down the fag-strewn concrete stairwell. I close the door and return to my bed wondering what Mr Emery did.

So what? Well, I got out of bed feeling alarmed, yes, but mostly I was curious. I'd walked along the hallway quite freely wearing only my underpants, and I'd opened the door without even asking who they were. I wasn't scared. I wasn't stuck stiff as a board under the covers, my stomach rigid with nausea, too scared to dial 999. That's how it would be now. I used to be the man I thought I was. It turns out I'm somebody I don't want to be. I'm going to burn it out.

Chrissy is making suggestions these days, in response to me claiming boredom with my job as the reason for missing work. This was one evening when I was hiding. She was saying:

'Why not try for your own place?'

'You're joking.'

'Not if you're as good as you say you are. You could do it.' There was no hint of any excitement at sharing a plan together. She was matter-of-fact, just trying to help.

'No money.'

'Find it.'

'I'm a chef, not a manager.'

'Get a manager. I don't know. Find a manager with money and make a partnership.'

'I could do, I suppose. It's not that it's impossible. I have got a name in the trade, considering my age. The trouble is . . .'

'What?'

'I'm in trouble.' Often I do this now. I come to the brink of a confession, to test the waters. Then I turn like a trout at the first sign of a shadow:

'What sort of trouble?'

'Terminal boredom.'

'Ah.'

'What?'

'I don't know the answer to that. Something positive like the Boy Scouts.'

Did Chrissy despise boredom? There was no sign of anything crossing her expression, nothing to imply criticism. She was smiling.

'I think,' she continued, 'that you could get help off some woman. What about Elaine?'

'Nah. Like blood out of a stone.'

'There's plenty more. One of them must be rich.'

'I don't want a restaurant. I don't know . . .'

'What do you want?'

'To escape. I want to escape.'

'Let's go and see a film then.'

'All right.'

So that night we went out. I uttered sentences wildly to her back as we crossed the threshold, and while I was turning the locks I thought, 'She's my guard, but she doesn't know it.' The difference was like a soothing chemical in my head, having her at my side. The Opponent was powerless, his defeat on this occasion turning him into a cynic, lounging against the broken lift. Bastard!

Chrissy has a car, and sliding into the seat next to her in the safety box I felt well looked-after. She was in charge. She drives fast, does Chrissy, no worries, except for her habit of cruising up to a stop in neutral. We were out and about like friends, but blinking a bit at the sight of each other in the unfamiliar neon. We went and saw a film with scenes of murderous violence projected onto a screen seven metres high.

February 22

We had a good laugh at me when they turned down my application to be an ambulance driver. Chrissy was there with a breakfast Item cutting up her orange in the usual segments.

The plastic table-cloth caught a stripe of the juice. Orange blood: thin and tart.

'God, why? Sounds like the dullest, most underpaid job . . .'

'I didn't realise about that part of it. They didn't tell me about ferrying the old ladies around for the first two years.'

They had told me, of course, and I'd been turned down even for that job.

'What did you expect?'

'I don't know. Something a bit more television, you know, a uniform, sirens, manic dashes through the traffic, saving lives . . . a radio pager . . .'

'All gone. They turned you down.'

'I'm not surprised.'

'Something else will come up.'

Chrissy thinks that I'm still working. I've told her I'm on the lunch shift, and occasionally I make sure I'm out when she comes back. The truth is, I've lost my position with the black-currant steaks. It was my best handle on this Life business, and my grip has been loosened and cast off. The idea of pretending to go to work I got from an alcoholic story: a man dressing up in a suit every morning for a year, leaving on the dot of the usual time, returning home with a loosened tie, tired, talking of the office. He had been free everyday to drink himself out into long-term senselessness, safe in his charade, until he ran out of money.

In a heave of effort to move the boundaries of my predicament I sometimes try and take the whole assortment of things that are happening to me, and play them off against each other, good ticked off against bad like plus and minus columns, to try and make up a balance sheet with a statement at the end. It's a pointless exercise. Nothing is put down here to add up to anything, in the conventional sense. There is another piece of news, something which should be a plus, but it doesn't make its effect. Chrissy and I have introduced ourselves, top to toe, physically touched along the whole length; we are lovers. That should count as a mark of improvement, to be held against my losing the job, but instead our closeness creeps round me like a conspiracy.

It's not that it wasn't an emotional experience; it was, in an unexpected way. No soft lights or music; it was in the cold baldness of the lounge with the centre light on, when she said:

'I think we could go together.'

I was pleased, I felt highlighted, pin-pointed in that wonderful sensorially intensified environment that such moments bring. The warmth bit, though, came later. We had moved, after a few more choice phrases to screen our embarrassment (like 'My place or yours?'), to my bedroom, and in the dark something dropped away: the cool woodenness from our expressions. Still with our clothes on we simply held each other, and she said:

'It's never any good the first time.'

For a long time we stayed put. My face was collapsed onto her shoulder. Relief, and relaxation, and warmth, and the novel shape of her body. When we began to get undressed I was cheerful. I said, 'Let's do the first practice.'

It's because I associate Chrissy with the Screaming Maisonette; that makes her part of the conspiracy. I am being led into something. I have no proof, but I believe my instinct. As I said, I'm like the donkey that's had a stick on its back, and then suddenly, suspiciously, it's been offered a carrot. This new plus in my life runs along the same lines, the same design,

except that unlike the donkey I'm not refusing to budge, oh no
. . . I'm running.

March 17

It was a good stage when we were both working. I was living
up to her, then, if only for a while. But now? It's not just the
shape of the flat that's changed with her moving across to my
side of the wall. There is an incalculable progress that's dis-
torting the mirror in which I see myself. This is an episode
from a week ago.

Chrissy is standing in the kitchen with her friend when I come
home. One of those times which go towards consolidating my
claim to be still working. She'd got back at midday, having
organised a half day off with her friend. They've been talking
all afternoon, and when I see them together they are enjoying
the air of conspiracy that they've made between them.

'Ah . . .' The friend looks at me with amusement. I ask:
'What?'
'Nothing. I know what's going to happen, that's all.'
Chrissy is looking at her friend and smiling. A sudden
wicked laugh breaks out between them. They are like witches.
I ask:
'What's going to happen?'
'Wouldn't you like to know.'
Again they laugh together. Chrissy has had her brown hair
cut shorter, but still it's a full head, a shiny bob. She is wearing
a short skirt as usual. Her legs fold well at the knee, cutting a
good line. She looks at me knowingly, as though I should get

39

this joke as well. Small chat continues with the friend. I'm not interested in trying to join in. They begin to ignore me so I go and have a bath. The murmur of their talk goes on secretly while I'm washing with the blue hippo sponge.

Her friend has gone, having given a polite shout of goodbye to me. Chrissy shuts the front door behind her and comes into the bathroom. I ask.

'What was all that about?'

'What?'

'What does she know that's going to happen?'

'You'll see.' She trails her hand in the water and makes circles round the top of my cock which is floating on the surface.

'It looks like a buoy, bobbing about in the water.'

'It is a boy.'

'Oh yeah, so it is. It looks dangerous, like a mine. Warn all shipping.'

'It'll explode if you touch it.'

Chrissy slowly lowers her head down towards the surface of the water.

'Warn all shipping . . .' She speaks softly, kneeling by the side of the bath and aiming for the tip that's growing out of the surface of the water. When she takes it into her mouth she swirls the bathwater around in her mouth and sinks her face carelessly into the tub. I lift my hands and pull her head onto me.

'This is what was going to happen,' she says later, when we're in the bedroom. I've already had enough, by now. She is looking at me steadily, sitting cross-legged on the floor. She has taken my hand and guided it between her legs. 'I want this to happen all night . . .' She rocks back and forth and stares at

40

my hand between her legs. She looks fascinated. My hand is a foreign thing working at her. She takes the fingers and helps them go faster and lighter. When she leans back onto the floor her head is in the cupboard next to the shoes. Her neck slides under the skin and arches up before she pulls me down on her. I am sending savage messages to my empty groin: 'Get up; get on with it; get hard you bastard; don't let me down; do it; fuck her!' When I come this time I am almost dry.

Later on from that, she's there in front of me, continuing to spread lotion on her buttocks. I notice the blotches on her face and neck, and the full flush on her chest. She leans forward towards me on the bed, dipping her back and still using both hands with the oil. 'Stroke yourself.' She speaks directly at my cock a few inches away from her. I take the battered thing and play with it while she looks on. It's past midnight, the diodes next to the bed tell me. Her hand pulls at my neck. When we are both on the floor and I am on all fours over the top of her another oily leg fastens round my back and Chrissy lifts herself off the ground. She is bucking underneath me. I try to enter her even though I'm soft. Her shoulders drop onto the carpet and she puts a hand down to work herself off. I masturbate up against her until she comes again. She blushes to the roots of her hair. I've never seen her do this before. It is like watching a medical condition.

It's hours beyond my bedtime when we are finally lying together quietly conversational, side by side in bed, and I'm exhausted with having lasted the distance. Chrissy has both of her eyes closed, one of them out of sight in the pillow. She mumbles monosyllables in response to my sporadic questions about her friend. Her mouth is set even more crooked in her face because of the pillow, trailing downwards on the right hand side, where I like to see it move. It captivates me. After a short time of staring into the darkness wondering what effect it would have, I say the sentence 'I lost my job.' There is no response. I imagine the words reaching her on the edge of her sleep. From that distance any words are warm and comforting. Either that or she's awake and doesn't want to talk about it.

Right now it's raining hard and I'm sitting in the lounge watching it, safe, this side of the window. The rain washes the dirt out of the sky and away down the city drains. The roads are streaming. In the middle of the road one object is left: I've worked out that it's a woman's black leather boot. It looks tiny from the fifth floor. It's made out of a cow's skin.

It's becoming automatic, how things read to me now. Unavoidable. I see the cow clumsy and frightened at the death-smell of the knackers; the bolt against its head in the crush, dropping like a sack after the bang, its skin being pulled off, cut up, and a small part of it, the underbelly maybe, turned into a boot. The girl is wearing the boot in his car. The car pulls up, and the girl gets out, or she's thrown out, and she curses and slams the door. A corner of her fake fur coat gets caught. The car takes off fast and she gets dragged. The boot falls off when she's given up trying to get to her feet . . . and so on.

I have a pen and paper and I'm sitting at the table. It's time for the exam. *Question 1:* 'State exactly what it is that makes you afraid. You are only allowed to use one word, to avoid generalisations.' This might be unfair. Surely if you use only one word it's more likely to be a generalisation? No matter. We know the answer – 'The Opponent.'

My Opponent first appeared outside the front door shortly

42

after the Original Incident. It was a legitimate invention. After all, my attacker had my name and address from my wallet. I am still fully expecting to see him on the other side of the spyhole. The substitute, the invention, my 'Opponent', was merely put there to preclude any surprise. If you expect something to happen, it never does, so it was by way of a fervent expectation. Of course, in the beginning he was wearing a camelhair overcoat, and carrying the sprung steel Item in his pocket. I imagined him lounging outside the front door, often blocking the stairwell by leaning the length of one arm against the wall and staring down at his feet. He hardly looked at me at all. He didn't need to. It wasn't long before I deduced that it was him that was leaving all the cigarette butts in the stairwell, and from there it was only a short step to click that it was him that put the lift out of action every bloody day of the week. However, after a while this invention changed. He became more than just a direct figuration of that Item's pending arrival; he changed character. This was due to a fright I had one night.

I don't know why I woke up. I was looking out from my bed and what I was seeing in the darkness of the hallway made my eyes stir quickly into wakefulness. There was a tall hooded figure standing just beyond the bedroom door. Imagine it, as I stared harder to make it go away, the figure resolved into a clearer shape. He was very tall, that's for certain, and completely black like a shadow. I couldn't see a single contour of his face. He wore a hood that sloped down onto his shoulders and a cloak that fell to his feet. He stood perfectly still. After a while I realised that he could not be human. No one could keep so perfectly still for that long. I cannot imagine being more awake than I was then. My elbow was nerved up so much I could hardly lean on it. I stared. I was seeing my first ghost. That's when I thought, 'This is my Opponent.' I looked so hard at it that the shape swam from the force of my concentration. It was exciting because it still stayed there. I tried to communicate with it, expecting a hollow voice to reply in my head. 'Who are you?' I asked, urgently. 'Are you the Opponent?' The figure stayed impassive. The night gained status. God, to think that I'd conjured up this figure!

It was not the end of it when I realised that the bedroom door was actually shut and the hooded figure 'in the hallway' was made up of the dressing gown and towel hanging on the back of the door. The figure made his mark. He makes a more suitable Opponent. He encompasses more than the Item. He is more symbolic. He has acquired a melodramatic stature, posing outside the front door. His face, when he lets you see it, appears from out of the hood all made up in white powder. He's tall. He wears pointed shoes. He always looks at me directly, and his gestures are large, simple, slow repetitions. When I open the door he raises his hand slowly, the palm flat towards me, at the same time raising his eyes to meet mine. When the palm of his hand is level with my face it stops. He shakes his head, mocking sadness.

The bit of paper with my first exam question on it has got covered in large black question marks, so I've thrown it away. I took the paper and tore it up into small pieces so that Chrissy couldn't possibly work it out.

Needless to say I am a success at my own exam because I am marking the paper. Unfortunately that's not good enough. Chrissy is my examiner. I must come up with an answer that'll pass with her. She doesn't even know that the question needs to be addressed. Not yet. I've come near.

She looked at me in disbelief because I suddenly started crying. I sobbed unwillingly, feeling the shame of them as they bubbled out in front of us, sudden bewilderment pushing them out. With my head buried in my hands I gave vague incoherent excuses, bits of the truth dressed up and presented as monolithic world issues: 'The world ... so much hate ... look, on television ... nothing but conflict and war ...' She was to admire me as oh-*very* sensitive, but instead she was surprised. I saw it pass across her face before her duty became clear to her. When I was cleaning up and still snivelling, I felt glad that I'd cried. It would pave the way to a meeting-place for our understanding. She would no longer be surprised because I could tell all. We would begin to connect. She would love me.

April 15

This is what happened last night. It's enough for me to say that I retrieved all the warmth I was talking about before from this. It's only the second time, but our relationship isn't that old. These two times, when we've floated ourselves off on a peaceful, good-humoured, ordinary romance; they have only been allowed to happen when the circumstances have conceded me *safety* ...

We are in Chrissy's car near Button Hill. The light is failing. She's driving fast and repeating the words 'Oh God' over and over in mock horror and embarrassment. Her skirt gets impossibly short when she's driving.

'Oh God!' she cries, letting out a long groan of mock death. 'Who was he?'

'It's the car. He recognised the car. Why did I have to wind the bloody window down?'

'Not rude enough.'

Her hands are quick on the wheel, but she gives a slight wag to the steering every time she changes gear.

'What did I say?'

'You were very friendly.'

'Oh no! I was startled out of my wits.'

'You told him he was welcome any time.'

'Oh Gaawwd!'

She stops the car. Button Hill looms up dark on one side. Chrissy stares, holding her bottom lip in her teeth. She looks over her shoulder as if he might have followed the car.

'What a horrible bloke.'

'Who is he?'

'He knows me from work. He's a Greek. A businessman. Retailer. He's quite good, as it goes. Never have any trouble from him.'

'What's his name?'

'I can't remember. Something Greek.'

'Mr Popupandseeme.'

'That's it! That's the one! Mr Pullhisknoboff.'

We climb out of the car. Chrissy locks the doors. Our hands swing easily together across the road to Button Hill.

Chrissy says, 'He's a Popupandseeme bloke all right.'

'Is he married?'

'Don't know.'

'He's probably got some poor slave at home. Imagine being married to him.'

'Mrs Popupandseeme? I doubt anyone would do it.'

We break hands to begin the climb up the path in single file.

The damp mud and the grass feel suddenly treacherous; they are enemies of us city people. Chrissy goes first.

'Mrs Popupandseeme sits at home surrounded by wall-paper.' She speaks over her shoulder, toiling upwards.

'And Mr Popupandseeme comes home and says, "Hello dear."'

'Hello Juicy. Her name's Juicy . . . Juicy Popupandseeme.'

'Hello Juicy . . .'

We are getting near to the top of Button Hill. I am still having to follow Chrissy up the winding path. Her skirt has a brief cut in the back and the two corners have curled out: triangular flags waving at me one at a time with each step up the hill.

Chrissy says, 'Imagine the knob on it.'

'I'd refuse to touch it.'

'Revolting. Like a green chilli I expect.'

'Like a saveloy sausage without the skin.'

'Ugh . . .'

'Probably always damp with sweat.'

'Shut up.'

'Soggy. Bent in the middle.'

'Shut up!'

At the top of Button Hill we stop and look at the view. I am relieved that the Greek was known to her through her work. The argument runs comfortably through my head. He couldn't have had anything to do with the Screaming Maisonette. I can poke fun at him quite easily. He's far removed from any threat.

Chrissy turns and hangs off my neck like a tired weight. When I feel her fingers tickling the back of my neck I know it's on for a Go at the top of Button Hill. The view of London is blocked by her hair. While our hands are moving over each other's bodies the night is closing. No matter the damp ground. It's spring.

April 30

My first real decisive attempt to get out of it has been determined by a chance opportunity. Chrissy has been expecting that I will get another job soon. I have talked about a few mythical offers, always saying that I'm turning them down because they're not good enough. Now, I really have got something to try out, and I had to sell it to her.

Even as I said it I realised full well that I was doing it this way firstly to hide myself. Secondly it was a bid to make it more interesting to her, my unknowing adjudicator. I refused to tell her anything.

'I'm in trouble.'

'What sort of trouble?'

'I can't tell you. It's nothing too serious.'

'Is it dangerous?'

'No, not really.'

'Is it money?'

'No.'

She is furious. 'Why? What's going to happen while you're away, that's going to make it all right to come back?'

'I can't tell you.'

'Look . . .' she says. Her weight is slumped sarcastically on one foot. While she waits for the words she places her hand in her hair. 'Look . . . if you want to leave me say so and fuck off. Don't tell stories.'

48

'It's not a story.'

'It sounds like a story.'

'I don't tell stories.'

'You're a good man at your job. You know you could get work any place. So why the hell down there in the bottom of the country?'

'It's not a story. I might have to go away for a couple of months. This is the only place I could find. I can get a proper job when I get back, no trouble. All I want is for us to make a deal.'

Chrissy sits on the sofa. One leg is folded underneath her. She is fiddling with a piece of something.

I say, 'It's only maybe. And I won't go unless we make a deal.'

'What happens if I don't make the deal?'

'I'm in trouble.'

May 5

Mr Popupandseeme came the other day. He looked enormous in the spyhole. He entered the place as though it was a hotel foyer, saying he had something to leave for Chrissy. He sat underneath the Dali picture. It was awkward because we didn't have anything to say to one another. I should have refused to let him wait. He didn't feel awkward. He took it that this was a waiting-room for Chrissy, and that I was her flat-mate. The Dali picture made a comment on him. If you pulled out the drawers in Mr Popupandseeme's stomach you'd have a job to close them again what with having to push all the hummous and the kebabs and the guts back in. He looked at me kindly.

'It's very good of you, you know, to do what you've done for Chrissy.'

'Oh?' I say, thinking of our jokes against him. He seems harmless.

'Taking her in . . . into your own home . . . very good.'

The conversation stayed there. I went to the kitchen to make a meal. Chrissy and I could eat it when he'd been got rid of.

In the kitchen I hung around doing nothing. I was fingering things, and thinking of Chrissy's fury at the mystery I've created for her.

It's strange to see my set of Items in their wooden block here at home. They are razor-sharp. For some time when old Pop-upandseeme was there I drew them out and slid them back into their respective places in the wooden block. The blades are heavy and silent.

I can hear the double click of the spring-loaded Item in the Original Incident. The memory of the sound tics against my nerve. It's like the static slip of electricity between your finger and the metal banister in a hotel lobby.

Later, after he'd got to see Chrissy and hand over the flowers and do his brief flurry of polite compliments and invitations and a big smiling farewell, Chrissy said to me:

'He is an automatic man.'

'Automatic?'

'Yes. God, it's bloody mad! He doesn't see me for ages. He comes into work all the time and doesn't bother to say hello. Then it happens again! He hears that I'm no longer with anyone. Ten minutes later he's there! Ready to be my best friend! Ready to take his bloody trousers down and declare undying love! He's on automatic, that guy.'

'We're all on automatic. He's just simple enough not to hide it.'

'Speak for yourself.'

'You were on automatic just now. Look how friendly you were towards him. All sweetness and light. As soon as he's gone you turn him into a zombie.'

'He is a zombie.'

'I thought you were going to invite him to eat.'

'I managed to get off before that.'

'Thank God.'

Chrissy looks at me from behind a forkful of food. Her long crooked mouth turns down at one end, and the tongue flicks out. The food goes in and spills down her chin. This is the cue for her imitation. She chews on for a while, noisily. I can see the food in her mouth when she speaks. It's a hoarse rasping voice with a bad Greek accent: 'Very good . . . very good grub. Well done! Well done, Juicy!'

I think, 'I am an automatic man, stuck on a different switch.' There is no logic, that's the frightening part. Rational thought doesn't count, doesn't have any effect . . . I'm in with Mr Popupandseeme. I'm stuck here now, switched on, but not allowing myself to jump off the balcony. But there's too much at stake not to try anything. So I'm going to leap as far as I can. I'll make the deal with Chrissy. Then I'll spring myself. Get right out of it, get myself a good escape, something that works. Then I can come back and try to deal a straight hand with Chrissy. As long as I don't leave her behind, as long as she makes the deal, I'm going to leap as far as Cornwall.

Two

July 2

Cornwall. South Coast. Village life is hidden. How do people mate in the country? Perhaps a brief sighting, and then an attack like wolves in the forest round the back of the pub. Either that, or a million 'Good mornings' to the milkman finally culminate in a weird stumbling kiss and marriage. The tourists are doing it on the beaches.

I live in a room upstairs, above the tea-house and shop. The room is dry and salty with very cheap curtains running along a plastic-covered wire. My bed is an iron school bed and the only thing that's not square in the whole room. I miss my pictures.

The tea-house has dried fish exhibited on the walls. In the middle of each table is a hard brittle sea-urchin. (Dead.) Sea-urchins have pride of place with the salts and peppers and sugars. There is a very unhygienic-looking cat wandering freely through the premises. I am not at the peak of my profession.

The owner is not difficult. He doesn't expect much. He finds objects which interest him, and politicking means examining these things he takes from his pockets to explain to you, and sharing his wonder. If only he was better at surprises, he'd be interesting.

London is very far away. Here it's the ground under your

feet, the Earth. I've never felt this. I lie down in the field and spread myself face down. My chin is wet in the grass. My arms and legs are wrapped round the surface of this gigantic planet. I have a huge ball in my hands, a ball so big I have to hang on while it spins carelessly fast. I close my eyes to feel the rush through space. I'm riding through the passage of one day like it's a fairground thrash.

Fear Index: 0. (As long as I don't think of London and Chrissy.)

July 10

It's very quiet. When I get up, birds are speaking outside the window, which makes it seem quieter. I am alone in the building. There are virtually no customers in the place until 11 a.m., except the odd doddering pensioner after a bottle of milk at the shop. Opening the door in the mornings is when I look for the difference. Is the Opponent going to follow me down here, and lurk outside my cheap room? Would he have a country outfit, or still the same old cape and hood? I can laugh in his face, now, because he is nowhere to be seen. I left him at the top of the stairwell in London, I think. He gave me a last glance after I'd barged past him, his cynical eyes following my attempt to journey beyond his check. Here I can walk out every morning and the only reason for any excretion of adrenalin is the sense of space. It takes off, travelling away from me. The pattern of hedges condenses when you follow the perspective, and then the whole lot disappears over the edge of the cliff, some two miles away. I must walk it to find the detail of what I'm looking at.

The owner still comes to pass instructions over. He gives them away like the things from his pocket. He likes to talk to someone. He doesn't mean to be pedantic.

Today I feel the routine begin to grip.

Fear Index: 0.

July 18

Another letter from Chrissy. They look very sophisticated down here, the grimy London postmarks, lying amongst last year's leaves in the post box. She accuses me of being evasive, impersonal. It still rankles, this mystery flight to the country.

I walk the scrubby pasture fields early in the morning before work. There is no necessity to stick to hedgerows because there aren't any crops to trample down. Nevertheless I creep round the edges to be able to watch the rabbits. They look perfect and fresh in the damp grass. Perhaps they grow overnight like mushrooms. I wear dark clothing to get closer, and then stand stock still. The early morning is their slot, their time of day. They are calm but watchful, always watchful, while they shuffle-hop and eat seriously. Occasionally they afford themselves a moment of play.

Of course, as I stand motionless against the hedge, I am thinking of them in relation to my own preoccupation. They live under constant threat of being shot at or eaten alive, yet they still manage to find courage to come out into the open for a while. At any moment a man could lift a gun to his cheek, and the familiar noise would rip another disaster through the fur. They are watching constantly for the first sign of that animal with the long jaw and rows of teeth as it runs a fierce line towards them, when they have to split in all directions and try to swerve off line to avoid the catch of the bite on the back of their necks. They have infinitely more reason to be afraid than I do. To be run at by a whippet must be the equivalent of being chased by an express train. They are alert, always listening, always watching, because they have come to an understanding. Death is always ready to tip the balance. Nevertheless they have small moments of peace, and they accept these quietly before having to escape in blind panic to save their skins. They don't question it. They don't think.

Fear Index: 0.

July 30

Gordon and his nanny come into the shop again at five in the afternoon. They are the only light relief in the course of the day. The brat Gordon begs to be entertained. I don't blame him.

Life in the tea-house reassures me with a pattern so staggeringly ordinary that it seems forced out of a time stretched twice as long as anywhere else. In medieval tapestries life is portrayed as a sequence of actions leading one to another, frame after frame following on with new scenes, new accomplishments. Here is Harold mustering his army to fight off the threat of the Nordics; here is Harold commanding his foot soldiers into action; here is Harold holding onto an arrow that's stuck into his eye. There must have been a terrorist amongst the tapestry-makers, a woman suddenly forced by frustration to protest: threading up a new picture, that of herself achingly bent over the weaving mechanism, and then

55

repeating endlessly over and over again the same picture of herself, at last content that she is portraying life as it unfolds in front of her.

The pictures of my own life would make up a couple of frames: unloading a tea-tray in front of the stodgy tourists; washing up; serving in the shop; stretching up to the shelves; dabbing at the till.

(July 30 p.m.)

It's hard to believe, but I'm living in a tea-house and shop close to the coast of Cornwall. I am living without fear in an environment devoid of threat. Even at night, like now, when the silence is hung on the trees, I could go downstairs and walk with the huge night passing by on either side of my face. I'm a free man, unharmed.

However, I'm unable to ignore Chrissy's letters, which lie in a pile on the square bedside table. She would have sat down every now and again and written them on the plastic tablecloth in the London flat. Little white messages sent through the hands of strangers. Chrissy and my Opponent beckon me. They have no intention of leaving me alone. They are always there in the back of my mind, both issuing an accusation. My Opponent is standing in his hooded garb, displaying himself aggressively at the top of the fag-strewn concrete stairwell, mouthing words that tickle the back of my neck: 'Come on then, it's all very well hidden away down there amongst the pensioners! Do you dare come back here? I am waiting for you!' His white face is ridiculously affected. His teeth look sordidly yellow in comparison. 'I am waiting for you with the two specific Items, you know, the two exact things . . . !'

Fear Index: if I stop thinking, 0.

August 2

The rabbits still hang out in the same corners of the same fields. They seem quite happy. It's obviously better not to think at all. I am fascinated with the idea of 'not thinking'. I think a lot about it. But in the end it's impossible. One can't be like a rabbit, or like a lion, just by trying. One has to deal with oneself. The only way of 'not thinking' is to think of something else. If an iron-toothed monster is eating your balls, it helps to bite your lip. The working day stretches ahead of me. Thank God for the working day.

Fear Index: 0.

August 5

The owner tries to get out of me why I am here, a person of my credentials. I tell him it's like a holiday and he smiles approvingly. He takes the necklace out of his pocket and asks me what I think it is.

'It's a Star of David.'

'Oh.'

'Not so many years ago this could have killed you if you'd got it out of your pocket in Germany.'

'I s'pose that's right!'

'You're in the right place at the right time.'

Fear Index: 0.

August 6

I am turning back from my walk when the tentatively peaceful atmosphere of the rabbits is broken up by a terrible screaming noise. A cat has got hold of one of the smaller rabbits and is reaffirming its grip on the poor animal's neck. The piteous high-pitched scream ends abruptly and the upside down legs give a last twitch; and then the cat drags it clumsily out of sight. I return here feeling a bit numb. If I had to fill in the Fear Index now I'm not sure what I'd put. It could be a question mark, or nothing at all.

(August 6 p.m.)

Our cat, Lawrence, drags the young rabbit in under his chest, bringing it home to give to me. He puts it down by the geranium pot outside the front door. It's missing its head and one leg.

Fear Index: = Stupid Idea.

Three

The old man with the collapsed mouth doesn't need a cup of tea. Nevertheless I deliver it in a flowery 'china' cup (unbreakable). I wish for a moment that he could have collapsed over the threshold of the tea-shop croaking and tearing at his throat, and when I lean over him I think I can make out the words '. . . tea . . .' This old man doesn't need tea, he just needs to forget that he has nothing to do but wait for death to come and poach either him or his wife. He's afraid to admit that life is tedious and pointless and *very nearly finished with*. I take him and his wife their tray, and unload it carefully while they watch my hands. As I plant a scone in front of him I say:

'Battered bowler hat, sir.'

It's a strange victory to take over a defenceless old man, but it's a start. He can't understand what I've said, and treats it like a spoon has just dropped off the table. Absurdity isn't absurd to him, it's only incomprehensible.

He's afraid of the blank empty space when I take the finished cup away from in front of him, so scared he has to get up and go. He is scared of his wife's arthritis, reminded by the messy expression on her face as she tries to rise. He's not scared of her death, but she might have to be looked after, and she's ugly, old, decaying into humourless folds of skin, and their time together is worn out. He receives some help from pretending to believe in God, and some solace from the fact that he owns a house and a car, but it's a pathetic defence; I can see defeat in the pompous way he pays the bill.

In my salty dry summer room I am listening to the radio and thinking of the usual things. I catch the middle of a sentence: '. . . symbolic of the things that live in dead wood . . .' and then again, 'dead wood . . .' and again it comes, '. . . dead and decaying wood . . .' Even such an *innocuous* sentence springs at my throat. No! I am not afraid of dead wood, or even of death; I could commit suicide with quite reasonable cheerfulness. What I am being forced to look at is the fact that things live on dead wood, that they require the wood to be *dead* for them to *live*. It is the horror of the predicament that I am now being continually forced to recognise.

The fact that our cat Lawrence brought what was left of the rabbit to my doorstep puts me irrevocably in the picture. Before, I felt the victim of an obsession; now I see myself as part of a Hierarchy of Fear. I am not at the bottom, but somewhere above the rabbits. A mood is settling over me. My mind percolates always, in the end, towards revulsion. A thought can begin anywhere, but it always discovers the same results: despising and hatred. I despise the Hierarchy of Fear. Man eats cow eats grass eats earth eats man. It's all so unconscious, so very established. The humble worm has the most pathetic deal – no eyes no ears no teeth etc., just given the last mouthful, clearing away the left-over morsels of debris to allow the whole cycle to start again. It is the set pattern of existence, set like a bad habit.

I feel bewildered at my place in the Hierarchy. As a species, as a *Homo sapiens*, I am meant to be at the top of the Hierarchy, with almost any animal at my mercy, from a wild boar to a rabbit, but I can only believe that my own fear, my own portion of that universal emotion, is much larger than any of theirs, and larger than most of the rest of my species.

Perhaps therein lies the secret strength of *Homo sapiens*. We are so afraid that we are forced to stretch to brutally ingenious lengths to ensure our supremacy. If someone hadn't already done it, I'd start inventing a gun right now. It seems reasonable to suppose that it was fear itself that screwed *Homo sapiens* to such a pitch that it made him extraordinarily brave.

I tread the lino along the same stained footpaths. The passageway between the shop and the tea-room has become narrower, and I am familiar with each corner of dirt. I know how to wriggle the plug on the kettle until it works. I know that some of the scuff on the walls has come from me. When I wipe down the surfaces and the sink at the end of the day, I know which bits of dirt are impossible to move. I know to watch the flap of lino in the doorway of the kitchen; it'll trip you if you don't know. The cat Lawrence moves round from window-sill to doorway to window-sill following the sun. Gordon and his nanny appear early in the mornings. I pursue my adventure with Gordon's nanny. The owner appears on Fridays to take the money. I masturbate occasionally over Chrissy, who is refusing to visit.

A new resolution takes time, time spent repeating the same moves in the argument as yesterday. A new state of mind is being laid down. It is formed in layers, definitely; made up out of sifting thoughts which, if there are enough of them and they are left undisturbed, harden into a resolution. The Hierarchy of Fear is being straticulated.

Gordon's nanny is in her teens. She has a soft outline of brown hair and a white shirt and a dress; and brown eyes that breed kindness. She would give her heart away willingly and genuinely, and then be surprised when she looked down and found it had gone. She wouldn't blame you, but she'd hate the sadness so she'd never do it again. Gordon is a small boy that she's employed to look after during the summer holidays. We have found a way of entertaining Gordon that makes him look forward to coming in the shop.

'Morning Gordon. What's it going to be?'

'Peaudouce nappies Peaudouce nappies!'

'I've got something better than that . . .'

Every day now for about a week Gordon has become one of the articles on the shelves. It started off down the bottom end of the shop with him being a bag of dog biscuits. His nanny would have to 'buy' the dog biscuits and she could then take Gordon off home again. We flirted, the girl and I, while Gordon thought he was the centre of attention. She is very young, and obvious like a meal on the table. The game with Gordon has become serious. Every now and again I've put him on a higher shelf. He has progressed from being dog biscuits through to soup, toiletries and Peaudouce nappies.

Now I take him, the squealing boy, under my arm, and lift him up the ladder to the topmost shelf where the boxes are kept for stocking up the shop.

As I descend the ladder I can see his eyes darting down to the floor below. He is giggling nervously, pressing himself away from the edge of the shelf. He is thrilled by the terror of the edge and the height above the floor. When I reach the floor I talk to the nanny and he stops giggling to listen. He needs to know how much she is going to have to pay to get him back, and whether or not she has enough money.

'That's it for today then,' I say to the nanny, 'time we were off home.'

Gordon shouts a complaint. We are breaking the rules. I take the nanny by the arm and lead her behind the counter and into the tiny loo at the back where the brooms stand. We stand together, embarrassed, in a sudden sexual heat. She is beginning to smile just before we kiss. I can hear Gordon start to get worried. Why weren't we buying him? His shouts turn to silence as I undo the buttons on her white blouse, and smell her under-age skin as new as a baby. Her breath heaves in surprise, and Gordon begins to cry from the shelf, scared he's going to fall off. She shudders, from the hips outwards, and pushes me off, fiddling with her buttons. Maybe the boy would tell his parents. I follow her into the shop. The boy is lying down on the shelf, hanging on with his mouth twisted and blubbing. He is only just a little bit above our heads. I climb the ladder and persuade him to let go and hold onto me instead. When he reaches the bottom he runs to her skirts, still crying. Then he turns round, absolutely delighted. He lets out a great gasp of triumph, his eyes bright as buttons looking at the shelf where he'd been, laughing at me and shouting, 'Again! Again!' I feel sick with the little brat. It's all part of some perverted pattern of instinct.

The next time she comes in there's no surprise. The two of us are in a conspiracy now. I tap the giggling Gordon on the head and say:

'I'll just put this box of sugar on the shelf.'

'And then can we go home again?'

I relish the fact that she's asked that question.

'Oh yes. I'm looking forward to it.'

Gordon is standing very straight and square with his arms rigid against his sides, doing an imitation of a box of sugar. I pick him up and climb the ladder to stash his nervous little body on the same shelf. I take the nanny back into the square room with the brooms in it.

She sits on the plastic loo seat. Gordon is still laughing hysterically. She leans forward and asks what if customers come in. I lean over her upturned face and she accepts my kiss. Gordon is calling; there might be customers waiting. She touches the front of my trousers very softly with her lips. I am surprised at that, and feel my groin clench with worry. She is undoing the buttons of her own shirt as I hold myself ready for her mouth. As she takes it in, the boy on the shelf in the shop begins to sob. I feel like crying too. It all seems so sad, looking down, watching the softness of her affection translated into this handling of the human sewers. I feel painfully detached. There has been some system of pulleys that's lifted my cock to meet her; I've had nothing to do with it. I think of performing some kindness for her, perhaps I could plant a bed of nasturtiums in my navel for her nose to sink into on each downward glide of her softening mouth. The noise from Gordon reaches a new pitch, and she breaks off. She looks up and smiles at me with opaque eyes, holding me to her breasts. I hear Gordon crying as though he's a long way away. She gets up to go and rescue him, smiling self-consciously. I look down on my cock as I try to pack it away: it looks like a vegetable just picked after a rainstorm, smelling freshly peeled and too big to fit in my trousers or her mouth.

A vegetable cock . . . those nasturtiums – this is life in the country.

So we can't finish our activities in the square room behind the shop. The explosion is left subsiding in the bottom of my groin as I follow her. She looks at me, appealingly. I've got to climb the ladder to reach the snivelling boy.

The disappointment drifts up to me, but it comes to me second-hand, like an object from the pocket of the shop owner. ('That is interesting ...') There is dust all over Gordon's hands, and the sound of her kind voice.

If we never saw each other again it would be a memory handed out between us. If she hated me now it might make my left ear burn. If she loved me she would be unhappy. Meanwhile Chrissy is miles away and doesn't know a thing.

Outside the shop we stand awkwardly but humorously and make a rendezvous for a night together.

As I kick my heels waiting for customers I think about the range of objects on offer from the pocket of the shop-owner. There was Worry, for a while, at being discovered. There was Vanity, all the way through as usual. There was Affection, and Sadness, and Cruelty. All regulation issue for the human being and nothing to do with me. Anybody could have them. I'm not considering myself as an individual any more. I'm an automatic man. It is the beginning of something, like the first strange hairs on your body. Menace.

I stand at the end of the driveway waiting for Gordon's nanny. Her figure solidifies out of the gloom and I see she is carrying the blanket. I am thinking of Chrissy, of the deal we've made for the summer. The Deal. Like Nuclear Disarmament. I'll withdraw mine if you withdraw yours. After the deal comes the problem of verification. Chrissy would have to be looking down at me through an infra-red spy satellite, watching the approach of the nanny with the blanket. The darkness suits Gordon's nanny. It makes her even softer round the edges. We don't say hello because we're meant to know each other better than that.

In the woods the spy satellite would see the two blurred outlines merge together. We embrace, while the blanket edges down the hill on a cushion of dead leaves. For Chrissy looking at her screen, verification would be complete; but I know better. I kneel astride Gordon's nanny and she pulls at my back.

'Your weight . . . your weight . . .'

I press the full length of my body along her and we hold like that, squirming as we kiss. I stand then to undress. I am looking down at her from a great height; she has raised one knee. Above me the deciduous trees hang heavy with summer greenery, darkening the night. Above them, Chrissy's satellite is having difficulty getting through. I can see detail. Her leg drops open still bent at the knee; it's luminous and white as only a girl's thigh can be. Her dress is lifted up the hill underneath her hand, her other hand reaching up; my hand taking it, my other hand lowering down to rest flat on her belly; surprise at how hard it is. The challenge of a brand new shape and texture of woman. I feel like listening to music – some grand voices threading through the trees with long vibrations of stringed instruments grinding at the heart. I would dissolve in passion; I want passion and sadness. From very close I can see how her leg is perfectly angled onto her body. Her hands pull me up and reach for the traditional iron-hard rod of trickery, but it's still only a limp cluster, like strange fruits left

66

too long hanging on the tree. I knew it already, but she is surprised. After the pause she bravely carries on. I say:

'I'm sorry, Chrissy.'

'What?'

'I said I'm sorry.'

The pause was back from before. It was the same one.

I said, 'I need a small boy to be crying in the background somewhere.'

Four

September 16

It's tea-time in London and the news is on the television. A daily round-up of horror and suffering transmitted on the hour to every home in the country complete with video pictures. There is a pecking order to the ugliness. If the war-torn ship is sinking in the South Atlantic there's no chance of getting the child-murderer in; if the fifteen dead in the coach crash hasn't happened yet we'll have to make do with the child-murderer. Today a woman was lucky to escape a lorry that ploughed through the wall of her living-room while she was watching TV. She was sitting in the armchair, probably watching the news, when suddenly the news comes hurtling through the wall instead. I am grief struck; afraid at the beginning and at the end, revolted.

I am waiting for Chrissy to come home; it's five minutes yet. Strange that I feel nervous, like she's a visitor who will find me with nothing new to say, nothing to show since the last time I saw her, which was this morning. I am a let-down, inevitably, at this time of day. I ought to be out. If only I could try and be outside somewhere, at any rate for half the time, then she would be a let-down.

I have had one victory over the Opponent since my return. When I opened the door, and saw him there with his cloak, holding it out like a Gothic matador with abrasively polite

68

manners, I simply retreated; I shut the door and stayed in-doors. I liked the look of surprise on his face; I just caught it as the door closed between us.

It's because of Cornwall and the discovery of the Hierarchy of Fear; that's what gave me the inclination. To be able to face him without clamping my teeth . . . to defuse him . . . Things have settled, gravitated down behind the teeth, sunk to some-where more central, perhaps an inch below the navel. I am scared. I accept. You don't have to tell *me*.

I won't tell Chrissy about Gordon's nanny. Why should I? It's nothing to do with her, except that it would cause her suffering if she knew. You can well imagine the scene if I went up to her and said out loud, "I seduced Gordon's nanny." It would be an act of cruelty, like walking up to her as she sits naked in the bedroom and cutting her tits off.

After that it would be hell. To go up to her in the ultimate privacy of our bed, to rest my head on her shoulder, would be like screaming, "This is the head that did it. Look, here it is, there's no guarantee!" If she decided that she was going to ignore the pain, beat it off, it would exist to spite her, like a stone in her throat. She wouldn't be able to remove it with reasonable thoughts. It would defy both of us quite easily, growing harsher in the battle between us. I won't make her a victim. One in such a small flat is quite enough.

I hear the keys in the locks and the familiar echo of the concrete stairwell. Then comes the horrible rasping voice: 'Juicy . . . Juicy, where are you? Where's my tea? Where's my sticky tea? Juicy . . . ?'

As always it strikes me that Chrissy's appearances are ac-companied by a presentiment of danger. While sitting calmly in my chair watching television I am struck down.

Chrissy and I still haven't shaken ourselves down properly after the summer. The other day she came in with an idea for the kitchen. I replied:

'It doesn't matter. I was given the paint free so I used it. It would be nice to see it a new colour.'

She must treat the place as her own home. My spirits sank. Paint the kitchen. I surrender.

She had flopped in her chair as usual. She grinned at me and winked. I thought, 'She's happy ... ' It made me proud. I wanted to find out what she did in the summer.

'Make the tea then.'

When I came back from following her orders I saw her fiddling with some things on the mantelshelf that I had unpacked the day before.

'Tea ... '

Why was she fiddling with these things? I was reminded of a pair of dogs sharing the same basket, trampling all over the bed so they could lie down afresh. The two of us are still locking in together.

'Thanks ... ' she said. Should there have been cake as well?

I wanted to inject something into her, to surprise her, to stop her dead. I couldn't think of a way to do it.

I came back to London on the train, thinking often as usual about the Original Incident and the two Items. Sitting opposite me were an American couple who were of course talking openly and freely to everyone. They were retired, they were from Wyoming, they had no children. They looked around, smiling, perhaps expecting a firework display at any moment. After a last check that nothing was happening in the carriage, the male leaned forward to stare at me with a secret smiling expression fixed firmly on his face. Then he took out his wallet, extracted a business card, and handed it to me, tapping it and exclaiming, 'That's me!' The card had on it a line-drawing of a man sitting with a fishing rod. 'Albert J. Dexter.' Around the picture were printed phrases: 'No Job – No Money – No Phone.' I tucked it away in my own pocket. 'Thank you,' I said, 'that should come in very useful.' The American slapped his leg and laughed into his wife's face. She laughed right back at him. I had nothing but admiration for the old couple, but all the same I could have grabbed hold of both his cheeks and shaken him: ' . . . for God's sake look, can't you see?' I would print my own card. The picture would be of me looking out of the window again. But then I thought I wasn't doing a proper job on the Americans. I was behaving like one of those stingy priests who only see things through one pair of eyes, and consequently queer everything with their horrible marble stare. The two Americans were a mystery. I wanted to be inside their heads for a while, to see how the sensation was different. I was a scientist, for a moment, before remembering the depressing thought that my Opponent would almost certainly have taken the trouble to come all the way to meet me at the station, holding out his hand to help with the cases, right there at the very door of the bloody carriage as it pulled into Paddington station. At that point I was travelling backwards, probably at more than a hundred miles an hour.

I thought of another ruse to confound my Opponent; but this one didn't work. It was to be put into practice whenever I had to go out, and I had considered every movement. It began perfectly. I got to him quickly, before he had time to step forward, and took the cloak off him. Not too much of a snatch, just a calm lift before he had time to hold it out, and then I

71

swung it onto my own back while delivering a so-what expression directly into his eyes. This should have had the desired effect and left him shamed and redundant, but instead, after opening his eyes very wide, he rubbed his hands together and looked pleased. At the same time he changed suddenly, maturing dramatically, stooping over his curling hands. There is something going on with him. I am uncertain . . . When I returned he was holding a large pair of very blunt and rusty scissors in his hands. He took the cloak off me, hurriedly, and settled down in a crouch to work at it with the scissors. Now there are small tails of string and thread littering the ground around him. He is angling the scissors this way and that every time I open the door. He takes no notice of me. What's up with him? What's next? His behaviour is spoiling my resting-place in the Hierarchy of Fear.

September 20

Slowly, yes, but Chrissy and I are finding a place for each other again. We might be at the mantelshelf, leaning; in bed, matched front to back in a foetal curve; in the kitchen, working, looking down at the surfaces. Often there is avoidance going on. We watch each other. Warily we move around the three rooms of the flat, having thought about where the other one is, what they're doing, and what to do as a reply. We make up a diagram of mood and movement in three rooms, in a form endless and repetitive like Asian music.

Last night, the night I had the dream, we hung out together talking desultorily, when Chrissy came up with this, which caught me out, and made me feel bad. She was sitting as usual on top of one of her own feet. She asked me:

'Are you upset?'

'No, no.'

'No talk for me tonight. Talk to yourself Chrissy. Hello Chrissy, good day at work? No, foul. Really, why?'

'I'm not upset.'

Upset, like a barrel of apples? No . . .

'You've changed. Definitely.

'In what way?'

'You're quieter. You're not so eager to please. You don't want to show off so much.'

'You're not a tenant any more.'

'No.'

Although she couldn't know this, it was a bit different: it would have been more truthful to say that I'm not treating her any more like a gift from the other side of the spyhole. She is variously labelled as conspirator, spy, or judge.

A pause before the main bit of the conversation carried on, and I was thinking about why the spyhole is a horrible tool. Your friends appear as monsters, distorted by the fish-eye lens, and then the monsters know that you're scared because you use it before opening the door.

She was making no noise, except for the thud of her cup on the table every now and again. When I turned round, she was holding her tea to her lips, and then afterwards she looked curiously flat like a passport photograph. She was pressing into the back of the chair, staring at me. It's because she wasn't blinking, that's what made her seem like she was in a photo-booth. Then she spoke.

'You are not happy with me living here.'

I reply mechanically, 'I am.'

'You're not.'

'I'm not happy full stop.'

'What about?'

'Coming back to London.' I remind myself of my original exam question, but I'm way beyond that now, somehow.

'What is it? What's the problem? Why did you have to go in the first place? Have you got to go off on another secret bloody mission?

'No, no. I need to be here in London, really.'

'Why?'

'I don't know, but I do.'

'D'you want to split up?' Everyone has to use these words sometimes. It's like using a public lavatory. It's depressing. You've just got to get on with it. Don't blame her.

'No. Please, no.'

'I'm invading you, aren't I? That's what you think. I feel like a battleship.'

'You are a battleship. A great big steaming battleship with flags, and men on the deck waving, and big guns, covered in tarpaulin.'

'I'll leave then.'

'But I asked you in. I want you! Please stay berthed in my bed.'

'As long as you stop watching me like that.'

'Like what?'

'Like you're expecting me to hit you at any moment.'

'All right, as long as you stop watching me like that.'

'Like what?'

'Like you're going to hit me.'

'We must stop all this aggressive stuff. Battleships and hitting each other. You gave me a spy satellite last night, with infra-red.'

'I didn't think you were listening to that.'

'I was.'

I thought she'd been asleep. Why did I mention the spy satellite? Because it's painful avoiding honesty. You want to dive into it, suffering vertiginously until you do. Also, it might have been something a bit nastier that I was playing with. That business down in Cornwall has given me something, an incident, which I could use like ammunition. Something I've got tucked away in case the threat of her potency gets too big.

During the evening I made a check every now and again on the position of the moon. It's being drawn up like a silver coin on wires.

I am driving a jeep recklessly fast alongside a wire mesh fence, faster and faster. The ground is a blur only inches from my bare face; I am leaning over the front of the jeep. It'll crash if I don't control it. (Watch out for the fence.) I lean hard over to steer the jeep, the ground fanning my face as I ride the corner. I have to hang on using every muscle; my body is sticking to the jeep like glue.

Ahead of me there's a jumbo jet burning on the runway, lying askew and broken across the landing lights. It is covered in patches of white foam, like meringues, charred at the edges. There is water all round, although I can't see any; I can smell it. Probably being used to douse the fire.

Where is the jeep?

On the opposite side of the fence people are waiting, looking at the burning jet. I walk over to them in my bare feet and open the gate. I am in charge. I step forward, but they remain the same distance away from me. I step forward again, but still they are no closer. I have to get them through the gate in the fence. They're all in a queue, waiting for me. I step forward several more times, without success. I mustn't waste energy; it's urgent. Turning back I see the gate is closed, but it's easy for me to open it. I stand by the gate looking back at the queue. They exasperate me at a time like this. Why do they all look so glum? It dawns on me that they'll come through the gate if I turn away.

Further along the fence I am walking. It's dark, but I know that the fence is there. I can't hear the sound of my own footsteps any more. Another gate opens, and someone is coming through the gate towards me. I can't see them in the dark, so I stop dead. I wait for a long time, listening, staring into the darkness until my eyes hurt. It's flat black darkness all around. I hear something; it just catches me, I turn an ear sideways. It was an echo. The sand slips away from beneath my feet, and in struggling to regain my balance my knee locks up solid. I feel the sand trickle very slowly over my feet, displaced by the weight. I'm stuck. I hear the echo again, from a different place. I turn towards the new echo. It's frustrating because I know it's not where the Item is, it's where he isn't.

All at once, in the straining silence, a switch is thrown. Sudden noise. I can hear a mix of breathing, blood pumping, and the sand settling dangerously.

I listen to the noise. He's very close, almost on top of me. I reach out a hand. As I breathe in, I hear the suck of air.

The moment I realise I'm listening to myself my heart rate increases. I have to control the sound. I squeeze my eyes shut and feel that rising feeling of hysteria that my brother described so well. I weep, out of control, trying to calm the noise down, trying to affect it in some way.

It's him ... he's eluding me by using an echo. I am stuck in the sand trying to control the noise. I must escape. Is he an echo ... ?

I am convinced that he is cheating.

76

Let me give you an idea of a typical morning.

If it is Tuesday morning we have already dropped our dressing-gowns and dressed to sit together properly over breakfast. The sun glares hot and watery through the window making the plastic table-cloth tacky. Chrissy fiddles messily with fruit. I am trying to avoid having to accompany her down to the tube station.

'I don't see why you insist.'

'Well, I do.'

'Why?'

'We're living together. We might end up walking around seeing exactly the same things for the rest of our lives if we always stick together like glue.'

I found this argument in a book. It's easier when someone else has made up your lie for you. Chrissy says:

'We don't work together.'

'No.'

'We'll see the same things anyway. The same street, the same houses, the same tube station.'

'I'm struggling for independence.'

'All right,' she says, her mouth smacking and releasing an orange pip down her chin, 'all right, that's fine by me.'

When Chrissy goes I look out of the window. People are walking to work. Some of them I recognise. They are five floors below me bobbing along the pavements like clumsy ants. Soon Chrissy will be amongst them. I wish her well, and find myself issuing a series of instructions to her when she appears: 'Cross over before the Alley . . . don't look at anyone for too long . . . be ready to run . . . '

Ten minutes after Chrissy has gone I open the front door. Crossing the threshold is like stepping into the foreign land that you've visited many times before.

Going down the staircase I listen to my own echo. My shoulders aren't feeling wide enough, my knee joints are vulnerable. The blocks of flats stick up like rotting teeth. On the corner is the Screaming Maisonette, just the same. I run the screams as usual. Chrissy, or, to be accurate, a woman, maybe Chrissy, screaming, screams that tighten my gut, and I can do nothing because I'm afraid. I start walking again. Even now, I look at my toes and my stride bounces higher. I think, 'Stinking coward, you . . . '

Every time I put Chrissy's face behind the scream I have to remind myself that I can't be certain.

I imagine the scene, of course. She will be cowering against the kitchen units, he will be knocking her with the back of his hand. He would be an Item.

On the turn of the corner you can see the full length of the road ahead of you. These are the instructions. Stay on the right-hand side to avoid the Alley. The Alley excretes litter. As I draw level, I give a quick look down it. There's a million dark nights ingrained into the dirt on its walls. You can see as far as the dip in the middle where it goes under the railway line. Always at the bottom of the dip there is a puddle of its own juice, thin and suspicious. At night it glitters.

Beyond the Alley cross to the left-hand side to be close to the industrial units. A few people are on the pavements moving in both directions. Each one of us advances with a circle of space around us, an exclusion zone that takes a real effort to maintain. Usually it fails before the main road because of the increasing number of people. Search the people. They give off

78

their messages; from quite a distance you can tell whether to cross the road or not. Check the broken glass in the gutter. Signs of blood? As people pass, the Shortest Possible Glance for each of them, into their faces. Read their intention in just a flash of a second and then look away. Keep confidence in your own walk, even though your nerves have already run off.

Thank God for the women. They pass by like proud oases. Perhaps they are scared of me. An old lady stops up against the wall, watching as I pass. She blinks, looking at my feet. I think, 'I could rush up and tell her it's all right; stroll home with her moving at her slow pace talking about the old days. At the end of the walk I would give her a present of money that would double her pension. She would look at me, as dry as a walking stick, her life rekindled.' I follow along a stupid track like that to get away for a bit.

There are more people moving at the bottom of the road as it joins the main street. I've lost my exclusion zone. It's a relief because it's less effort. I'm in amongst the criss-cross flow of human beings. Turn right at the bottom, heading past Brown's Café. The Greeks are frowning and operating the till as fast as possible. Past Eurospares. Then under the railway bridge. The card shop's on the corner. My favourite card reads:

Thank you for taking enough time to care.
Thank you for caring enough to understand me.
Thank you for understanding enough to love me.

I like this card because it's displayed next door to the butcher's shop, and it's satisfying to think of people buying the card and then carrying on shopping next door, where the lambs' heads lie in a small parade in one corner, dumb and sightless, and the denuded pigs' feet, bundled together in clusters, hang without movement. I think of the rabbit. An immense volume of cruelty is being unloaded from a halal truck, stinking, without ceremony.

A traffic warden might afford me a brief flurry of hatred. She stands with one overworked leg skewed out at an impossible angle from the knee. 'Masochist,' I think, as she writes the number.

In the market the stalls are in full swing. It's very crowded with all the queues getting in people's way. I can expect a feeling of humanitarian goodness now. Here we all are, selling and buying, struggling on. A man talks in a confident voice about the special scissors to a small audience. He is auctioning. The whole walk through is blocked. I know some stall holders. I might nod or raise a hand or say a word of greeting, like I hadn't a care in the world, like I had very definitely somewhere to go that morning, somewhere important. A charade, every time a charade in the market. I stop briefly at the gold jewellery stall and scan the display, meanwhile fingering things that I have no intention of buying.

'Interested, sir?' He is fed up with me, but maybe I'll buy something one day.

'Well ... there's a birthday coming up ... I'm looking for something ... '

There's no chance now. It's too long after the Original Incident. Somewhere, someone is wearing my chain round their neck. I feel good leaving the stall. The pace of my walk is artificially slow. People watching me might think I'm on drugs.

Finally I reach the tube station. The walk has taken me

twenty minutes, ten minutes longer than Chrissy. I have to invent lies to avoid walking with her, because I go the long way round in order to circumnavigate the place where the Original Incident happened.

Where do I go on Tuesdays? To the Acupuncturist. There are three of them in white coats, and one of them's mine, to help me for half an hour. When I was there for the first time he gave me a thorough questioning. He asked me what I wanted from acupuncture. I replied that I wanted . . . that something had happened. In these rooms where people moved calmly and listened attentively I felt it wasn't allowed to say that anything was *urgent*. It's true that he looked like he could understand anything that I might say. In the end I boiled it down for him into something vague: there was this pressure, and it was only that I wanted to stay where I was, that I didn't want to be moved by a pressure . . . It was a confused interview, and I repeated myself. The pressure. Take it away. I don't want to have to go with it, or to shore myself up against it. He asked me to explain and I mumbled vaguely and unfurled my hand in the direction of the window. Then his knuckles were on me and the high-strung pain of the needles came. One by one. Pressure inserted to subtract pressure. The truth is that it's not out there, the other side of the window. The Opponent came in and put it on me; but not with needles.

The Opponent came into the flat. There was no knock, or warning, and I was embarrassingly naked. You know how you always think you could avoid an accident? For instance, surely, if you were about to have a smash in a car, you'd have time to put up your hand on the dashboard and save yourself from going through the screen? As the Opponent walked towards me with the wretched-looking thing in his hands I thought, 'Aren't things happening slowly enough for me to avoid this?' What you don't take into account is the unavoidable weight of your own body, and the inevitability of its processes. I couldn't move out of the way. The Opponent was waving the scrubby hacked-together waistcoat, and he wasn't bothering to conceal his excitement. As he tugged my arms through the holes, only managing it after several nervous old-man efforts, I noticed that he must have used some of his own clothing to make up the garment. He smelt different too.

He was looking at how the front did up. There were no buttons. Several scraps of string tied it together. They were not evenly matched on each side, so the cloth was rucked. A lump, a stiff seam of glue, lay under my armpit. One side was tighter than the other. The entire thing was damp against my skin, and tied up tight.

For two hours I sat and stared at the Opponent, who watched me steadfastly in return, waiting for signs of change. I was concentrating fiercely on fighting the irritation, growing familiar with the rubbing points. Each breath dragged my skin against it somewhere.

When I got to my feet the Opponent matched the brief explosion of movement exactly. We stood, turned in on each other. His cape had fallen off. Because of the sudden surprise of what I saw, the spell broke and I left the flat to get away from the transformation.

As I rushed out I felt dread. It wasn't going to be how I'd planned. I'd seen myself as growing familiar with my place in the Hierarchy, laconically accepting my fate, perhaps developing a type of small-time charm from my physical cowardice. Instead I am being goaded.

He wasn't a man at all. He was an old woman, but crackling with new energy. When we stood up to face each other the ragged remains of the cape dropped away and I recognised her. She was the sort of frail and raging old lady that you see suddenly standing up in the background of televised boxing matches, inciting the contestants.

It was because of her that I went to acupuncture. I put myself up for it because I was looking for something to soothe the exacerbation of the glue and the pins and the string holding me in the waistcoat, but instead there was an unexpected and irreversible drawback. The very first time I was treated revealed the mistake I'd made. The needles acted like draining rods. They pierced through some block in my energy course. When I left the building I was only able to reach the ground with the balls of my feet. Any more energy and I'd have flown like a charged-up kite.

No more acupuncture – I can't risk having any more energy. I will deal with what I've got by using it up on my new job. Burn off the virulence with hours of work.

In the kitchens I am busy giving orders. It's a relief to get them over and return to the speciality for the lunchtime birthday quartet booked in with their own menu. Salmon and Celery Remoulade. Now I have my mind free. I look at the Items, my own set, used every day. Somehow they're all the same; I could slip and cut myself; it often happens, even in professional kitchens.

I unpack the salmon. A perfect specimen, fresh, complete. I lift it from the box of ice, squeezing the chilled slithery weight of it. I love fish, as a food, both to cook and to eat. Fish have the strength of the perfect line. When I get them out I like to

83

bend them, to feel the power of their supple bodies. They are cold-blooded naked muscle, with the skin fitting tight. As I transfer it to the slab a muddy brown line ejects from its anus. It's good and fresh. I choose an Item from the set. The salmon looks gormless on the slab. It only ever had a small bundle of instincts, now killed off.

The Item picks up the edge of its gill, slips underneath, and crunches through the neck like it's plastic. It feels springy and fit. The eyes bulge and the mouth opens; it looks surprised. I feel a stab of sympathy. Opening the bottom edge of the fish I am reminded of an envelope. I have to get the guts out quickly to avoid shame and I resent the spill not being completely clean; the brown line at the back of the arch is sickeningly elusive. I'm going to hang on to this work for all I'm worth, but I might have to find a vegetarian restaurant.

Later in the evening I've had a bit to drink. The sous-chefs keep a wary eye on me, since I was drunk once last week as well. I take the salmon's head and make it the centrepiece of an elaborate ice-cream dessert. Wafers fan each side of its head like a ridiculous collar. The waitress takes it and is three paces into the dining room before noticing the monster she's carrying. She dives back and rests against the serving counter, helpless with laughter. I feel refreshed, hanging on to it, and grin proudly at her streaming eyes until the very last moment of humour's gone.

The tube journey and the walk home. I feel weary, tired of resenting my condition. Perhaps I will buy a car. I remember again going to open the door to the two policemen in the middle of the night. I can't believe it. Half my brain must have been lying dormant.

The tube train rattles like a grown-up toy. An Item sits down

84

opposite me and stares into my eyes. Several Shortest Possible Glances, looking up from my book, tell me he is purposeful. I read the same paragraph over again. I'm stiff with terror and incapable of moving, like a rabbit pinned by headlights. But the sweat has soaked my waistcoat, and I'm being forced to think about fighting more than ever, at the same time wishing like never before that I was simply afraid and nothing else. Stuck in this argument, the most I can manage is a rather hysterical pretence that I am really interested in my book. Thank God for my book. Is a lion dazzled by headlights? The journey will last a long time tonight. I examine myself inwardly, and think, 'Force six.'

The word 'Item' comes from a long time ago. I never thought I'd use it again, but I dragged it up permanently after a sudden bout of thinking that night, way back, before the summer.

Imagine an artful little curve of tarmac called Elbury Crescent. Square houses were packed side by side along its length, with a bigger house at the end. Number one Elbury Crescent. This house had more prestige, of course, like the Sergeant-Major at the end of two rows of foot soldiers. The rest of us followed meekly behind, up to number twenty-nine. We were all bitter little ciphers, in that street, I'm sure of it. The boy opposite parked his Glo Truck next to his Dad's car in the garage. I'm sure all the kids tortured their pets.

'Item' was a word of secret meaning for my brother Paul and me. It's an ironic word now. Every time I use it it's like a kick on my own shin. Still, it works for me. This is how it came about, all that time ago.

Paul and I are avoiding the bloody grown-ups. They are worrying about installing a dresser complete with display of china in the corner of the hallway. They live a really boring life. Why the china? A ridiculous display. We'll never use it. It's there to fill the space. It'll be a real squeeze now, turning round the bottom of the staircase. Possessions and paraphernalia moving in bit by bit, each object creating three or four more 'corners' that need filling.

We have several rituals. The dalmatian is in the top-floor room and the grown-ups are out. These are favourable conditions. I'm off down the stairs (mind the stuff on the landing) to tell my brother that I've found the dog. That was no mean achievement.

'The Item!' exclaims my brother and sets off to get it from its hiding place. Not even I know where the Item is hidden. I might have cracked if I were interrogated.

Minutes later my brother and I climb the stairs to the top floor. Paul leaves the Item outside the door and we go in. The dalmatian refuses to look us both directly in the eye. It is about to be the centre of unwelcome attentions. It suspects that once again our relationship is going to be compromised by continued psychological experimentation. We advance into the room, and for now we manage to make friends. We engage the dog's attention in a routine game of jaw-slapping in the small corridors between the furniture. This is clean healthy fun, battling at ground level. Paul has left the room, but our pet dalmatian is watching my hands, trying to bite both of them at the same time as they come in to box his jaw. He is growling happily. What fun these humans are sometimes. Paul re-enters the room, hiding the old motor cycle helmet and the length of hosepipe behind his back. The dog glances at him, so I slap him in the chops to get his attention back. Paul puts the motor cycle helmet onto his head while I'm growling at the dog and getting both my hands bitten. The motor cycle helmet tilts forward, slopping about on his little-boy body. He leans backwards to hold it up straight. He looks like a toy. Then he drops to his knees and gropes for the hosepipe. The dog is still playing bright-eyed and happy with my hands. Paul stands up with the hosepipe hanging loosely at his side. It's going to be a megascare. With his unbroken voice hollowed out inside the helmet, he calls out:

'Bingo!'

The dalmatian whips round and on the instant it all becomes serious. He is barking to save his life, backing into me and hiding in amongst the furniture; he is trembling with anger, our dalmatian, furiously defending his position under the velvet chair. There is no fun now. His jaw is shaking because the fear in him is so cold. It's a deafening racket. Paul and I look interested. 'Force six,' says Paul from inside his helmet. 'Force seven,' I reply. 'That's probably enough unless we go in the garden.' There's not enough room indoors for a force eight.

Paul raises his arm into the air. That guarantees a force eight any day. Great. Paul and I laugh our heads off. We don't often do a force eight because it causes havoc with the stuff.

'It's because something happened to the poor darling,' says the gigantically well-hipped grown-up.

'What's happened to him?' I ask.

'I dare say he was badly treated by his last owner, who must have been a motor-cyclist. He came from Battersea Dogs' Home, and they often have hang-ups.'

She's proud of having done Bingo a favour. I say dutifully,

87

'Pity.'

'I think it's just a question of enough love. With enough love from his new owners, he'll eventually be able to forget.'

The sun is shining brightly at the height of its summer track. Paul and I are advancing towards the dalmatian at the bottom of the garden. We're hidden from the house. I can hear the distant clatter of washing-up chat coming from the open window. I ask Paul, 'What is it?'

'You'll see.'

'Is it new?'

'It's weird!'

The dalmatian is sniffing around the compost heap. It sees our approach and runs straight for Paul, jumping up onto his chest. He pats it vigorously. We really do love the dog; it's just curiosity. Paul holds out his arm stiff at the elbow and pointing down. The dalmatian knows the trick; you can tell he's done it before. It mounts his arm and starts humping its back, pulling the usual face: abstracted concentration.

'That's not new.'

'Wait . . . '

The dalmatian is making a really thorough job of it, staggering on its back legs and working contentedly.

'Watch out!'

'What?'

'There'll be lots of little arms being born.'

'Lots of little boys' arms with dogs' legs, running round the garden.'

'Weird.'

'Wei – erd!'

The dalmatian jumps off and returns to the compost heap, looking back over its shoulder just once. Paul turns to me and holds up his hand, spreading his fingers. There are lines of goo slipping betwen them; he's smiling.

'What . . . ?' I am aghast.

'It's easy.'

'How?'

'You just have to stroke it. It's like a trigger.'

'What is it?'

Paul laughs and runs off.

Elbury Crescent has the atmosphere of a Pony Club race. You have a house and you have to rush very fast to fill it with all the right things. First you have to get a car and start trading it in. Then you drop your kids. Then hurry hurry hurry, fit the kitchen – that's a difficult bit to get right. Just when you've got it done, oh, disaster! The husband has an affair and leaves home. Luckily the wife has a lover anyway who quickly moves in; not too much time has been lost and we can catch up if we go faster. Other people in the race see your setback and feel sorry for you. But they have to get on with the race themselves.

At night Elbury Crescent is quiet and yellow. Looking out of my bedroom window on the top floor there's not a sign of life. But the race hasn't stopped. No hint of a half-time in this race. Instead serious homework is being done. Repairs are necessary to vital equipment. If not then in each house there's a television reinforcing the rules for four hours. I have my own portable which I watch avidly.

We keep regular appointments with the dalmatian.

Perhaps the Item is hidden somewhere, the dog doesn't know where. We are in the room, both of us holding out our

89

arms. The dog looks guilty. It knows it's either going to be a pervert or it's going to be terrified, or both at the same time. It might choose one of our arms. The other one of us goes to get the Item, to see what happens.

Then we progress to a more sophisticated experiment. One of us already has the Item. The dog is found and carried upstairs to the top floor. Holding it in your arms with a firm grip, you open the door with your foot. Inside the room it is confronted by a human boy sitting in the velvet chair wearing a motor cycle helmet, with one arm raised, holding a length of hosepipe, the other arm held inclined towards it, palm upwards. You have to take care not to get hurt when the dog scrambles out of your grasp. We learnt to clear the first two landings of stuff before the appointments.

The dalmatian could never be sure. Perhaps in the velvet chair the human would be sitting with one arm upraised, and one arm extended palm upmost, but without any motor cycle helmet or hosepipe. Just an ordinary small boy with a nice trick up his sleeve. Sometimes the boy would have a cloth wrapped round his head, or a waste basket. The dalmatian would sometimes conquer himself enough to give us hope. We persevere. Statistics are compiled in a secret book.

Eventually the three of us have enough experience together to arrive at a satisfactory conclusion to the experiment.

The grown-ups are out. We're all gathered on the top floor. Paul is sitting in the chair, in Pose Number One, with Item. The dalmatian is scatting about under the furniture in a semi-circle in front. As usual he is making a furious howling racket, staring at Paul's outstretched arm which has the fingers moving in a tickling motion, the palm turned upmost. At odd times he is dashing closer. Paul waits, like a stone figure except for his fingers. The dog goes silent suddenly, and looks at me. I am impassive, waiting also. Our dalmatian growls and goes closer, growling louder and barking short single barks. We hold our breath. The dalmatian takes Paul's arm under his chest. I notice that he's not looking at either of us. His jaw is trembling. He lifts himself up the arm. I can see his teeth. Success! We have tempted the dalmatian into an emotional union with his own terror.

Five

November 21

Love really is questionable today. How cruel of God to invent such a gimmick to tempt us into the torture of childbirth and brat-rearing. It's an old chestnut of a theory, but there is something wrong with our love-life, that's why I'm thinking it.

It was a sad sight when I went into the bedroom the other night. I felt like laughing. I thought, 'She's bought them for me!' She was walking across the bedroom, making an effort at being casual and artless, sitting then at the mirror, dipping a finger into a pot of something. The pots are all neatly arranged according to size, perhaps, or their schedule of use. She didn't look at me in the reflection of the mirror. She would have done so normally, if it wasn't for the new undies. Two can play that poise game. I decided to take no notice either.

The theory goes like this: we are both of us being manipulated into propagating the species. The fact that I love the curve of her hip is nothing to do with love. Someone is winding the spring that will lift my erection. Then I'll be moved to give her the sperm that's needed to fertilize the egg. I can love her; I can find myself to be passionate, or I can persuade myself that I love her at the most mature and profound level, but if what's in the guts of the word 'love' is a trick then it's out of my control. We are simply two people, completely alone, of opposing sex, in a room together. The rest is just pure hype and trickery.

I settled back on the pillows and crossed my arms. I thought, 'Is this being defensive? Is this another power game?' I'm beginning to see everything in terms of manipulating the detail of our status respective to one another.

Chrissy, having finished with her pots, climbed onto the bed and approached on all fours. This was after her winter holiday last month; her shoulders and cleavage were brown with patterns of pale downy hair, fading by the day. It's a bit freakish for the middle of winter, to look like that. She had a hand on each of my legs, using them as tracks, walking slowly up the bed towards me. She accentuated the curve in her back, and she was swaying gently from side to side. She was looking directly at me with a serious expression on her face. She might as well have been a wild boar wearing a pair of suspenders. It made me want to scream and run out of the room, I don't know why. I would never have done it, of course. I just looked up at the ceiling and gave a laugh, feeling self-conscious. She stopped dead and removed her weight from my legs, and then I just missed catching her arm as she got off the bed. She unstrapped and unrolled the underclothes with her back towards me, throwing them off and climbing into bed quickly and without any grace.

'Chrissy . . . '

'Don't bother.'

'What's the matter? I just felt funny for a bit, I didn't mean . . . '

'You don't want me any more.'

I could at this point have started a row. We would have probed each other's faults (again) and then after a couple of apologies we'd have nodded off to sleep. Or we could have had a physical fight and maybe the sex would just have happened like it used to before. I couldn't decide what to do. Not deciding was my decision. I just sat there, and took my time not deciding. Chrissy won't have known. A wild boar wearing suspenders. I can do without that as a challenge.

What is she doing, this brittle-haired old lady, this Opponent of mine, bullying her way into the flat? I'm frightened at the things I have started to do, but it is her fault, she's setting my course. She is not going to allow me to indulge my position at the bottom of the Hierarchy. Her incitements increase daily, driving me out of any place of rest that I might momentarily find. She must have action, now. Turning my thoughts, my imaginings and dreams, is no longer enough. She demands a form of behaviour from me; I must give it to her, offer it like a sacrifice. She is testing me. It's like she's putting a fence before a horse; there are two options. Either I can leap high enough to clear it, or I can blunder into it at a walking pace and wreck it for her. This last option is the sensible one, the least that I can do before she'll loosen the strings on me. Then the pressure will fizz out from between my ribs and from under my arms.

The first hurdle she set me at was stealing a bicycle. It was the only inanimate object over which she demonstrated any excitement; her tastes are almost exclusively in confrontations with Items, which was obviously out of the question, too high a fence even to look at. Stealing the bicycle seemed the most insignificant thing, the very least that would do. The bicycle was the starting-point. If I could demolish my Opponent at the outset . . . How? It was like I wanted to close my eyes and steal it, and then open my eyes to find myself waking up from

94

a bad dream, released from all charges, left to myself with a normal blood-pressure and a sigh of relief, and then, walking down the same road, I'd see that I hadn't stolen the bicycle at all. I did try once to walk off with it, but on the point of engaging, I observed a strange notion come into my head that I should just lie down in the road hugging the bicycle in my arms and wait for someone to come up and stamp on me. Decided to climb down. I haven't even got the courage to fail.

Instead I turned over the Midnight Shop, sort of.

The Midnight Shop sells everything. The staff are easy to identify because they wear bright red pinafores. The manager creeps around in mufti, but he is small and can't look over the height of the shelves. There is one security mirror. I had devised my system, and spent some time getting used to it, intending that the staff would be unwittingly trained to allow me to get away with it.

Firstly, I always used my own bag instead of the wire basket. The first few times I did this the manager followed me round the shop and right up to the till, suspecting that some of his precious groceries were going to be swiped from under his nose by an unscrupulous Mediterranean-looking thug. At the till I emptied it all out, of course, every time.

I talked to the shop assistants. It's just the old ladies who bother to do that, usually. Most shoppers only look at the things they're buying being handled by the shop assistants, or they stare at the money they're passing over, hoping it will leap back into their gasping purses. So, I might say, 'Any chance of a discount, then, for students?' I would speak in a friendly tone, and afterwards add my own little laugh, the laugh of the non-villain.

God knows, I had to hang on to the best view of things, to

keep it light, so as to prevent pathos. How absurd my behaviour was becoming! If I had a wealth of courage I could do something big; the spastic old wrinkly would gorge herself until her goitres were full, and grow immediately fat on it, and retire. I'd get rid of her at a stroke. But you can't save up courage like coins. I said to myself, 'It's a mere token, but when she sees how poor I am . . . '

The manager was safely hidden behind the vegetable stall. The continuous muzak was playing as usual, stringing along with the danger in me. It underlined the petty misery of the place. The manager deserved to be robbed. That thin, snotty attempt at a moustache! My glance round the shop was not typical. I felt hunted. I passed by the video club selection. Perhaps this was going to be the beginning of my getting a starring role in the movie of the manager's life. *The Villain*.

I placed biscuits and fruit carefully on top of the newspaper. Beneath the newspaper was hidden the swag. I collected more things: a pint of milk, some green pasta, and, right in front of the manager, some tomatoes. I considered asking for his help, but I might have sounded hysterical. Anyway I wasn't supposed to know he worked there. Tension was making me overplay the part. I thought, 'For God's sake! Hang on to it normally! Pace yourself!'

When I was at the check-out, I still wasn't ready to make the decision whether or not to go through with it. I wasn't a thief until I walked out of the door, so for now I was safe to carry on.

I asked the shop assistant, 'What about a discount for people who wear green shoes?' The laugh of the non-villain came out a bit dry. There was a crack in it; you could hear underneath the hysterical cackle of the convicted criminal.

'You're feeling poor again then, are you?' she asked.

'Yes, poor again!' I noted with interest that I felt clumsy handling the groceries, and handing over the money. This could be dangerous; I would fall off the bicycle maybe. 'So poor,' I continued, 'that I have to steal groceries by the bagful. I've got a month's supply under my coat!' She laughed to give me a slight reward.

I wandered to the door. It was difficult to go out guilty. I faced inwards towards the displays, pretending to think whether I needed anything else. It was rather a ham performance, with a big show of deciding 'No.' Then I turned on my heel and walked out.

'Excuse me sir!' cried the shop assistant. The plan was to feign ignorance, but after all, I wasn't exactly surprised at the sensation of pleasure. I don't think I could have run anyway. I was overwhelmingly clumsy and hysterically happy, scarcely capable of stringing two words together. I also wore (for protection) an aspect of amiability – the affectionate smile, the willingness to lie down and have my stomach stamped on. I turned towards the sales assistant, breathless with extreme guilt. She was waving the green pasta. I went back into the shop and took it from her, and then I can safely say that the manager of the shop was truly confounded, from the top of his brown moustache to the tip of his brown vinyl shoes, watching one of his customers put everything back on the shelves.

When I got home I threw the empty bag in its corner and waited for a reaction in the kitchen. None came. There was no sign.

So there's another landmark now when I walk to work. It's after the jewellery stall, and in amongst the shops proper before the tube station. It's a shop operating from under the railway line, and it sells bicycles. There's a great confused crowd of them indoors with a gulley running down the middle. A few of the second-hand models spill onto the pavement outside, because it's got so crowded. A stocky man wearing shorts plies back and forth doing business. I've got to take him or fall; I can't refuse.

Some days pass bleakly, no matter what. It's as if they're determined from the start. Yesterday was such a day.

I was with Chrissy, on a day off, and feeling less than clear about my actions. A face in amongst a herd of other faces, all of us shopping, I couldn't ask any of them to untie my knots, even though I felt like asking everyone to have a try. It was a feeling of poverty in my character – I was not well made, a human being shabbily executed, flawed. I couldn't tell Chrissy about it. She was walking slowly, eyeing things in the shops a couple of windows behind me. I was stopped at the new landmark. The bicycle was still there. Three times out of four it is in the same place, in the furthest stand away from the shop door. It taunts me. There's no chain locking it to the stand. All it requires is a casual stroll up to it, and a quick but neat lift. I must remember to pedal off in the downhill direction.

It's a question of gathering yourself. My character has to rise to that level for only a few minutes, no more.

I was staring at the bicycle, while ticking off the things on the list that the Opponent had given me, all the reasons it deserves to be stolen: the Fornitto gears, the cantilever brakes, the alloy rims, the name painted on the crossbar. Funny, but she doesn't listen when I scream at her that I have enough money to buy the thing tomorrow if I want.

Chrissy was dawdling behind. She still wears a short skirt

98

even in this cold, but with a pair of thick tights underneath. Her body was hunched on top of the legs.

I took it into my head that this was the time to start on the bicycle. I was feeling discontented, so the best thing was to move on with the journey, to try and figure the next step. Build myself up bit by bit. I needed to get into the bicycle place to reconnoitre the layout, and to find out how many people work there, and what they're likely to see. I needed all this information to begin planning a system. When Chrissy caught up with me I said:

'I want to go in here.'

'D'you know Tony, then?'

'Who?'

'Oh. D'you want a bicycle?'

'I just want to look.'

She went in ahead of me, and when I lifted my head after negotiating the threshold I saw that she was waving at the man at the back of the shop. We walked down the gulley between the mess of bicycles on each side. It didn't surprise me that Chrissy knew the man. She knows many more people than me round here; she's lived here longer. I looked at the tilt of her skirt as she stood with her weight on one leg, waving an arm as she talked to him, something obvious and polite about the shop, I expect. Even so, there was the possibility that he might have been something to her once. I could see quite easily that the leg she was standing on could have, in the past, hiked itself up and swung over his back. He wouldn't have been wearing shorts then. Did her heel press into his buttock . . . ? It's of no importance anyway, but it was that sort of day.

I feel gloomy suddenly because I'm going to hang myself

crashing about trying to clamber over or wreck these fences that she's putting up. Is it possible to get rid of her, her with the smudged make-up all over her collapsed lips, to throw her off? I am striving to work myself up into being able to do that, so that I can return to feeling like an ordinary, uncomplicated sort of human being. I must remember to reward myself every now and again, to give myself encouragement.

My bicycle was visible from inside the shop. I could see the gearshifts mounted on the handlebars. Luckily, however, it is right up against the edge of any possible viewpoint. If I imagine myself now lifting it out of its stand, I'd be just to one side of the bicycle, and almost entirely hidden from anyone at the back of the shop. My arms would come into view, like so; and perhaps one shoulder and my hip. I must remember to keep my face turned away from the window. I will do it in the late afternoon, when it's dark. I'll approach, and swing the bike out of its stand and away . . .

I heard a burst of laughter from Chrissy follow on from the drone of his voice. I'd been examining the details, so I'd missed it. I turned to look at him. He was wearing glasses and he looked stocky and bouncy. He reminded me of the idiots you get in pubs. Chrissy introduced us then, and he gave my hand a strong grip. I thought, 'Is this a good idea?' After the introduction I checked my clothing: track suit and the sweat shirt with the Russian printing on it. I'll wear something different when the time comes. I continued to look round the shop. Somehow I must work out a system, to make it absolutely safe.

He was enjoying Chrissy. Often his eyes flicked down to watch her mouth while she was talking. I stared at her nipple, because I'm allowed to. I looked at his cocky profile as he

100

talked and thought, 'I'm going to rob you . . . ' I can picture him stomping back up the gully calling angrily to his mate. By then I will have stolen the second-hand Fell Rider.

When I had finished looking at a few bikes, my way of examining that outside corner a bit more, Chrissy and I turned and left the shop. We were an ordinary couple walking together.

The click of her heels started up again on the pavement. It was like walking next to a metronome. I was having to field the looks she got from other men.

The rhythm of her shoes broke when we hit the crowds. I had rubber soles so you couldn't tell. I thought, 'I'm a silent partner.'

On the corner by the traffic lights a baby was in a pram, and a large dog was approaching at a fast walk. The baby was staring at the dog, with its hands out to the open air for no apparent reason. The dog was set on its target. The baby's expression was fixed. The dog didn't slow down; I could see its nose inch out further to greet the smell . . . It walked right up, bumping its nose into the baby's eye, before walking on unconcerned. The baby's expression was still painted the same way. Two seconds later it crumpled and an explosion of misery came out of a suddenly enormous hole between its nose and its chin. I thought, 'That's only the beginning, you poor little bastard. Brace up!'

Later, when I've imagined an animal weighing forty-eight stone appearing from underneath the railway arch and bumping me in the eye, I realise once again my position as an automatic victim, switched on, as it stands, for really no great reason, when you think of the monster that the baby has just seen.

I put my silent footfalls in time with Chrissy's tapping. We were synchronised. I asked:

'Chrissy?'

'Mm?'

'Who was that in the shop?'

'That was Tony.'

'What did he say?'

'Just gossip.'

'What did he say to make you laugh?'

'Oh yes. That was funny.'

'Why?'

'Oh, I couldn't possibly tell you.'

'Why not?'

'It's a secret.'

'What is it?' I tried to bite back my interest, recognising the trap.

'You'd get into something that's too big for you.'

'Like what?'

'You might have to go away again.'

Chrissy enjoyed her revenge. I was hooked, even though I knew it was a game. She was doing it to spite me.

Chrissy's clicking walk was carrying us towards the place of the Original Incident. I said:

'I want to get something. You carry on. I'll see you in a bit back at the flat.'

The metronome quickened.

'You don't have to walk with me. Or I could walk with a blindfold, if you like, so I don't see the same things as you.'

'Chrissy, that's not what I meant . . . '

'Don't worry, I can do without you too.'

I stopped still, while she carried on towards the place of the

Original Incident. I wished with all my heart that I was in her shoes. She was clicking faster because she was angry. I was worried. She sounded like a bomb.

I turned on my heel, ready to take the long way. I'd have to buy something now to keep up with my story. This could turn out to be an expensive fib, eventually.

I feel much more in tune with the women walking along the road than with the men. The women look as though they're fielding the exclusion zone around them in order to feel safe. They look as I imagine I look. The range of the force field depends on the intensity of the danger. In the day-time in a reasonably safe place it might only be a simple circle of about a double arm's length all around us. In the night-time, in a dangerous place, it's as wide as we can throw it, and it sweeps up every side street in front and behind. With the Alley it's a bit different, of course; an exclusion zone is inadequate. The Alley is like a minefield. You simply avoid it.

The men are fielding something else entirely. I could easily herd up all the males together in a big cage, and then take them out and shake them one by one, shouting an inch away from their faces, 'Give it a rest, you bloody idiots!'

Men walking down the road are issuing a secretion which acts like an accusation, or a demand. They have measured the quality of their aggression, and when they throw it down at your feet they look to see if you can match it. This is the Test, and everyone is required to give an answer, even if it's only to say that you've given up.

The Test is not only a prancing war of aggression on the overcrowded streets. It's a thousand subtle social challenges.

These are some that I saw just on that one walk home alone yesterday.

The car going past has a V8 engine that sounds rich with mute power. It burbles like it's coming from under water. The driver has turned the stereo up loud and opened the windows. The music thumps and hisses a challenge to all of us within earshot. The driver has made sure to buy that particular car with that particular engine. The rest of us are excited. He's passed the Test; now he can despise those of us who haven't.

Meanwhile he's dawdling along in the heavy traffic. His head nods in time with the music. You can see it quite clearly. He's making up new Tests for himself.

As I am walking back the way we came, in the opposite direction to Chrissy, I'm thinking, 'It's in the brain of every single human male. Our thoughts are turned and twisted by the idea. There are twenty-seven million males in this country. The energy devoted to the Test is awesome; enough to suck the whole idea into a void. One day the Test will implode.'

I've been wandering around vaguely looking at things, and not even concentrating on getting home. I stop in the market and consider what to buy. I can't think of anything, so my alibi ends up being some fruit.

Just the posture of the man behind the fruit stall is enough. He has developed his physique. The raw man: flesh, blood and bone. That's all he needs, and the right clothes to show them off properly. Hours of work in a gymnasium are the investment. Now he can afford to be generous with those shoulders. We all of us notice, and secretly acknowledge. He has found his particular answer.

104

I take my own long-winded way home. Chrissy will be in the flat by now. My silent rubber shoes carry me along the familiar route.

A gang of lads are talking, sprawled on a low brick wall. I overhear:

'What she want with me? I don't want nothing to do with her. She disgusted me. She put blood on my sheet. I ain't askin' her back . . . '

I tick off the proof I need. The volume of the voice, the sidelong swivelled look to make sure I heard his gutteral cry, the magnificent confidence. I want it.

I am always trawling home through a sea of such incidents, all small, all normal, all gathering behind me.

When I'm about to dive into my particular warren of stairs I look up to the fifth floor to see my Opponent waiting behind the window. I know what she's going to do. She has a new trick. In her hand she's holding a little white silk glove. It looks rather crumpled and dirty as she waves at me. Perhaps she's been sucking it. I can't see her eyes watching me from this range. She looks like she's trying to say something, at the same time as waving the glove. I am so weary of her antics! She will make out that she has decided to give me the glove. Just as I'm about to take it, however, she will drop it on purpose, opening the fingers of her hand like a melodramatic magician. As I mount the sections of the concrete stairwell one by one, I am wishing that I could give her the weekend off.

Last night I was sitting in bed reading. I was feeling very pleased with myself because the day was over, and in fact it ended on not too bad a note. Thus, from time to time I was even enjoying being smug, because of my new 'picture'. It had

105

made me feel pleasant and, for once, safe. If only this warmth could be moulded and struck fast, instead of being as elusive and as sudden as mirth.

Then the door opens quietly and Chrissy appears. She's naked, and treads carefully, like there might be glass. She stops still, standing simple and unaffected, looking at me. For some moments we just stare. She says:

'I want sex.'

She doesn't sound raunchy, or humorous, or at all determined. She says the words like you might say, 'Please help me.' It's a pathetic sight, and I am helpless. I want to look after her, like she's just caught a sickness that I've given to her. I am responsible for her now. Still I feel the warmth.

I hold out my hand and she comes and takes it, so I make room for her to get under the cover. I feel touched. She's settling, and staring at me doubtfully, lying on her front, resting her head on an arm. I stroke her back. I always liked how well muscled she was. While she's trying to work out an answer I stroke her buttocks and my face sets into an expression of anger. She asks:

'What is it?'

'It's nothing, really. Nothing to worry about.'

I tighten my grip on the anger. It's the only thing that's going to stop me from laughing. I mustn't laugh, because of what happened before when I laughed. She mistakes the seriousness of my expression. She turns on her side and lifts her hands to her breasts, looking at me all the while. One hand she spares to explore me. It's impossible to say anything. I pull her quickly towards me and hug her very hard, whispering an evasive line of conversation. She is pinned down beneath my weight. I keep pressing us together, trying to think of a story

106

to tell. Nothing comes immediately to mind. It seems like nothing has happened to me so far this winter. Every day has been the same story.

I say, 'I've got a new picture.'

She gives no reply. I say:

'I'm sorry. I was just thinking, that's all. I was miles behind you.'

'What were you thinking?'

It's no good telling her about the picture. I'll have to think of something else.

'I was thinking about earlier today, when I was coming home by myself without you.'

'Why, what happened?'

'I was walking along thinking that suicide will be available on the National Health in future'

Chrissy is looking at my mouth. I feel like I must make it carry on moving.

'And various other things.'

'Why should suicide be available on the National Health?' She asks the question seriously.

'I was thinking of the old man who had his toe cut off by burglars. It was in the papers.'

'And?'

'I stood for a while on the little knoll in the park . . . '

She interrupts: 'What park?'

'Well, not a park, that patch of green.'

'Why were you coming back that way?'

'I was wandering a bit. Anyway, I stood in the sun on top of the knoll. Little kids were dashing in between the different bushes. They were whispering and excited. Then suddenly a podgy white one wearing glasses rolled out from behind a sapling, and came to a halt. He was pretending to fire a machine-gun at his enemies behind the bushes.'

Chrissy is inert; a substantial femininity, still in my grip. I don't know what she's thinking.

'Then a thin scraggy boy leapt out in retaliation and did an overarm throw, you know, lobbing a grenade and making the noise himself to explain it. Then all hell broke loose. Machine-guns were the favourite noise. They sounded like stuttery laughs, but with all the happiness taken out, and then injected with absolute seriousness. At the end the little fat boy lay stone dead. Then, when he'd finished having a great time lying still, and no one was going to come and get him, he jumped up and roared off. I came home. It was too cold.'

Chrissy asks me, 'Why did you tell me that? What point does it have?'

'No point at all. I was just miles behind. I was explaining what it was.'

'I'm not a child. Don't creep up to me. Why don't you just tell me to fuck off? What are you trying to do?'

She turns away from me and escapes to the furthest edge of the bed. Her shiny brown hair I can remember noticing the very first time I saw her, before we even met. Now it's all that's showing of her.

In the middle of the night I was still awake and looking at Chrissy asleep. As usual she was spread out like a corpse. I used always to think 'killed in action', but it doesn't really work any more.

I couldn't sleep because my chest was so tight. Every time it felt like it was contracting I realised that it was because there were two lungfuls of air under pressure in there that I wasn't letting out. I went and sat in the dark in the lounge, ready to travel more hours of time in front of the big window overlooking the city.

Spread out beneath the window in this room is the concrete pattern of my stomping-ground. I can tabulate all the landmarks from here. The Screaming Maisonette is almost right opposite, at one end of the low block that's in front of us, although well below the level of my window. The Alley is hidden as always. The usual scattering of litter marks its mouth, the descent into Hell. Even the foxes avoid it. The place of the Original Incident is also out of sight, but I know between which squares of concrete it's concealing itself. The bicycle is locked away every night just below the furthest yellow sodium lights. I see in my mind's eye the price tag turning in my hand: £200. Expensive for a second-hand bike, but why not go and buy it tomorrow?

The windows of the Screaming Maisonette were dark. One of the red and white curtains had been clamped in the window; the corner left outside was sodden. It's been like that for some time now. I wondered who was in there, sleeping, vulnerable. I have in the past seen the shadow of a human crossing behind the curtain. There was a red light bulb in the middle room, and the dark shadow looked devilish when it crossed the crimson background. I wonder if Chrissy has ever slept in that particular room. Maybe she was lying there being skewered by the man. I hate all those three windows. I hate the shadows that move behind them.

Thankfully, there is my new picture. I call it a picture because I have realised that it has reached that status now, but in fact it isn't a picture at all, it's a window-frame with a real living occupant. Further along in front of us, again at a lower level, there's a small square window with a red frame. There are no curtains. Looking down through the window in the day-time you can see a sink and draining-board. Always the same woman appears to work at the washing-up. She is big enough to fill the entire glass, and her arms move in a gentle rhythm – well practised, melancholic. When I wasn't working I couldn't believe that nobody but her ever came to that sink, not even to get a glass of water. There are enough dishes to clean for a whole family. She always comes and does the chore in just the same way. She rolls the sleeves up on her big arms, puts on the gloves, and away she goes, steadily working on a marathon of dipping and wiping. I want to meet her, but I wouldn't be able to recognise her because I've never seen her face. The window is too small; from this angle I can only see her torso and her moving arms and her neck, with a gold necklace lying there twisted, a tiny thread of good luck. Today I saw the winter sun catch that window and glaze it with gold. Last night when I was in here my new picture was black. The washing-up was done, I dare say, all cleared up. She was no doubt asleep somewhere in that building, a mountain of bed-clothes being lifted by her breath.

I was cold sitting in the lounge, but I wanted to hang on for a bit longer because I was so wide awake. To reduce the cold I was pressing myself into the depths of the armchair, with my body curled up to expose the smallest possible surface area.

The road below was suddenly no longer empty. One lone figure, a male dressed in black, was walking close to the wall. I know that feeling. He would have almost preferred it to be completely dark, rather than be picked out by the yellow floodlights. He looked fatally vulnerable, blocked in on all sides by the ugly weight of the concrete. He'd been channelled into a maze; the difficulty was not so much to find his way out of it, the problem for him was that the maze had been spiked with arbitrary and violent Tests.

I followed his progress intently. His hand was thrust deep into a coat pocket to make people think he was carrying a gun. He was walking fast, but none the less, compared to the vast map of the city that I can see from up here, he was making slow progress. A tiny figure in black struggling against the crimewave. While I was thinking that he was pitiable, he suddenly stopped in his tracks. I could see no reason. He stayed as he was for some number of seconds, then turned back the way he came, head down, walking the same snappy strides.

Then there came the growing murmur of a V8 driven through an automatic box. It came into sight slowly prowling along in the middle of the road. The man in black stopped and the car caught up with him, pulling in to the kerb. The engine idled, freed from the drive. The man stooped and talked into the car for several seconds, and then stepped back. The car leapt forward, and dived into the corner, the tyres just sounding. The man turned round once again to face his original direction, and walked quickly without stopping. I had just seen the middle of something.

It was difficult to tell whether the man in black had just passed or failed. But it seemed to me that he'd been walking on a high wire. Hunched in my chair, I considered the advantages of the V8 engine.

The pictures hanging on the walls were wide awake. They are old friends, those two; silent, fixed, forever intelligent. The Dali is absolutely certain of itself at that time of night. The drawers in the curved body are open for inspection. There is

111

nothing equivocal about its monstrous claims. The Chaissac, up at the other end of the room, is not so sure. The internal argument continues. The Chaissac would answer evasively if you went up and asked it whether or not seagulls shit peanuts.

I remember when I saw Chrissy for the first time. This would be over a year ago, now. This first sighting was followed by a couple of coincidences, and then some strange behaviour on my part. Anyway, that first time, I was walking home, just on the last straight before the Screaming Maisonette.

I saw the figure ahead of me bent double over its own knees, sitting on a suitcase, on the bottom step of the crumbly concrete staircase leading up to the Maisonette. A small figure, fallen into a huddle. I saw that it was a girl, dressed in a fashionable bulky coat and a short skirt. I would be passing in front of her in a while. She was probably waiting for a friend, or for a taxi. The stairs up to the front door of the Screaming Maisonette also lead up to several other maisonettes, but conclusions formulated automatically in my mind as I drew closer. When I walked past all I could see was that she had very shiny brown hair. Then her head started up. She had only just heard the noise of me passing. It was all part of the resident normality that her eyes were streaming with tears, and that her face was smudged all over with suffering. The conclusions that I had invented in my approach suddenly got scuttled, heavy with real potential.

When I was upstairs in my empty flat I could see her just round the edge of the corner, still sitting in the same way. I paced up and down in front of the window, checking frequently. I imagined the scene again in the Screaming Maisonette: I am walking past, and I hear a woman screaming. I'm incapable of going in to see if she needs help; my feet won't move, I'm rooted to the spot. She would be leaning back against the kitchen units, cowering, and screaming. The Item would be hitting her with the back of his hand.

Now I'd got a face, and with it the nuisance of pity, and the need to be brave enough to play the figure of mercy for the victim of the attack in the Screaming Maisonette. That face I saw turning to look at me. . . It had no mark on it when I walked past behind her, but it had been over a month since the Maisonette had screamed. The marks would have cleared, wouldn't they? I could now invent the sharp twist of the face as she spat at him; the blow coming fast through the air; the quiet, dull, unlikely sound of it; and then the swing of her hair is like a curtain falling on the scene.

I was so indecisive. I paced about, thinking that if I did go back downstairs and offer her help she would be frightened off. It would be ridiculous to call a cab for her. I returned from every excursion to various corners of the flat, after anything I did, to see that she was in the same position: I had dribbled the incompetent teapot, answered the phone, and wandered in and out of the empty rooms. I started to cook in the kitchen; I can remember not thinking about what I was doing. It was a long time ago, and I didn't know it then, but I can tell you that the motives driving my control of the events included wanting to put one over on the Screaming Maisonette.

After two hours she was still the same dot in the same position in my window. I had written a note to her. It offered help in any form – money, or a room to stay the night, or food, or someone to talk to. I sealed the note in an envelope, and addressed it 'In case of emergency'. I would go, and without

113

saying a word, simply hand it to her. Then it would be up to her.

After I had spent a further half-hour prevaricating, she suddenly disappeared. I was relieved, thinking that it was because she must be all right, her predicament resolved in some way, but of course I was relieved because the contest between me and those three windows had been called off. I tore up the note, thinking how stupid I was to have considered interfering. Oh yes, it was just the sort of careless bravery that could get me into all sorts of trouble.

It's a bitter reward, but a reward none the less, to see how naive I was then. I can believe, when I think of times well behind me like this, that I have made progress this year. Back then I was simply scared. I looked at myself and diagnosed the miserable condition I was in as a disease that I had caught. The moment of infection had been a pin-point of memory, a struggle, a sound, the running double-click of the knife appearing from nowhere, never seen, only felt, as it infected my blood with simple, uncomplicated fear. As for before the Original Incident, I hadn't even realised that I wasn't immune.

Now, of course, I understand more. It is not simply being afraid that makes me unhappy. The fear itself is not the thing that makes it sit on my mind day and night, aggravating me into my armchair in the corner. If I had a stem growing from my head, and a growth on top of the stem as big as the Chaissac, and I dragged the thing down in front of my face to see the colour of it, it wouldn't just be the colour of fear. There would be the colour of vanity as well. I am being cornered by the challenge to my vanity.

At times like this, when there is only a half-light eked out

114

into patches on the walls, my Opponent can work herself up into a grand fury. She stands there dressed in her nylon fibres, and the glove leaps into her hand by some trick or other. She raises it above her head to the fullest height, exposing the dreadful ageing harness of her underwear for several long seconds, and then dashes it so fiercely at my feet that it disintegrates. I am cornered. I am in the corner until I can pick up the glove. There is a constant barrage of Tests. I am trying not to respond.

December 8

I thought I had the perfect system for the bicycle Test. It did involve a small expense, but thanks to the market I managed to find a battered old gent's bike for £20. From my successful experience at the grocery shop I knew the importance of using a system to build up my own confidence. I looked forward for a while to the time when I would be able to develop the bravado of a simple thief, and that would be all that I'd have to do, that would be my answer. At the moment I am anything but cool and unconcerned about what happened.

In the early morning I took my bike out of the hallway and the first stroke of luck was that the lift was working. On the way down I felt extraordinarily unstable. The lift lurching into the start of its drop made me laugh, like a small and stupid happiness had managed to give a skip in the middle of my body. I was on the way to passing the Test, without, at this stage, having to be actually sure of doing anything. I rode down to the bicycle shop on the clanking, clicking old machine. Perhaps I would get my money back for it afterwards.

Outside the shop I realised that I was too early. The outside bikes had not been put out yet. So, in the café over the road, I stared over the top of the unbreakable teacup as the second-hand models were assembled one by one in their outside stands by Tony. He was wearing laced-up jean shorts again, with two or three scrappy jerseys to fight off the cold. If he was part of the old gang, then the old gang is not what I thought it was.

I had done the thinking round the problem of what to do with the bike once I'd stolen it. I decided I wouldn't use it for two weeks. During that time I would re-spray it a different colour. After that it would be OK to walk up to some nice spiky-looking kid and hand it to them as a surprise present. But what would I tell Chrissy?

Tony had reached half-way along the row, handling the bikes with expert quickness. He was short-tempered and dumpy in his expressions when he was lifting, probably because he was bored with his work. As I lifted the teacup to my lips I remembered the café in Cornwall and Gordon's nanny. It was a lifetime away. For the moment, while I was engaged like this, I was out of touch with what was behind me. It felt comforting, like the tea. I was suspended in my own operations.

I had thought for some time about my behaviour with Tony. Should I talk to him? Should I cancel the whole Test because he now knows me through Chrissy? I had come to the conclusion that it would be to my advantage to carry on. I would be the last person to arouse suspicion. I was quite sure that he would never be invited to the flat. I remembered Chrissy's casual attitude to 'the old gang'.

I have waited for Chrissy to talk about her past but it hasn't

116

come. I refuse to probe. Perhaps it will come eventually. I am forced to remember that she's not my property; she reminds me of that, even if it's been something as little as me taking out one of my moods on her. I always accede. I can still feel amazed at Chrissy coming to me like that. I want to disturb nothing. Our equilibrium is not self-contained, I have to be part of the effort. The small lies are for equilibrium's sake.

Tony took my bike out and along to the stand at the end. The bike was beautiful. I felt benevolent towards it. It moved next to him like a thoroughbred, ready to go. I would do only two runs to work up the system; then the snatch. I dreaded that the bike might be bought by someone, or worse, stolen from under my nose. I looked round the café as I stood to leave. A collection of men stared back, uninterested. I was the only one who was going to try and steal that bike.

I paid 25 pee and left. I took my own bike and pushed it across the road to where my victim stood looking proud and fast. I walked on for a bit because I needed to approach from a particular direction. When I returned, I swung my old crate round and organised it to lean very gently against the victim bike. If I reached out now I could touch it. There it was; the Test. I'd rather have dropped a brick down on the crossbar than let anyone else get it before me. I was moving with exaggerated care, because I was clumsy again, conscious of a burning in the back of my head as I imagined Tony looking at me. I walked into the shop, trying to pull off my gloves. Tony was at the bottom end of the gulley between the bikes, near the door to the office at the back of the arched building. My voice was uncooperative. Pathetic! What a miserable failure I felt I was on the criminal scene. I'd be an unhappy mug shot in a police file, with the nick-name 'Fumble fingers'. The file itself

117

would have a sticker with the title written on it: 'Small Fry'. Recklessly I carried on. After all, I was only buying bicycle clips.

Tony came forward to deal with me. He was wiping his hands on a rag. I greeted him:

'Hello. D'you remember . . . last week?'

'Yes. With Chrissy, wasn't it?'

'That's right. With Chrissy.'

We shook hands. I remembered the grip. It struck me that he was drilling himself. Perhaps he used to be in the army. His jaw was wide, and he was making an effort to stare at me. He wanted me to think I might be in line to get eaten. He said:

'She's changed a bit.'

'Really?'

'I thought so. Her clothes, her hair. Still the same girl, she just looks different. Then, I haven't seen her for a bit.'

'Did you know her well?'

'Nah . . . just an acquaintance. She's good. She's all right. She used to dress a bit more punky though, didn't she?'

'I don't know.'

'Anyway, what can I do for you?'

'I want some bicycle clips.'

Tony moved to the back of the shop. I turned round and looked out of the window. I could see my bike quite clearly propped up against the end of the row. I needed Tony to be watching me when I left. The idea behind the system was that if he saw me twice swinging a bike out from that position, then the third time, when my own bike wasn't there, I could walk off with the Fell Rider.

When I paid Tony for the bicycle clips he put the money straight in his pocket. I said thank you and he asked me to say hello to Chrissy for him. I agreed and left the shop, smiling cheerily. The first practice of the system was about to take place. It was simple: I took my bike and wheeled it away. I hoped he'd seen it.

I was guiding my own bike down the road just a few yards from the shop when I was pulled backwards off my feet. The bicycle dropped with a crash. Someone was gripping the back of my collar and an arm was round the front of my neck. Within the space of one broken moment my neck was being squeezed in a vice. I couldn't see who it was. I grew sick with panic: another attack from an Item. With one hand I was trying to break the grip, while with the other I was struggling to get my wallet out from underneath my overcoat. If he saw the wallet it would get the assault over with as quickly as possible. He was tugging at my head. The view swung wildly like when a television camera has been dropped. He had complete control over my body, pulling me over backwards, and then sideways over his knee. He reaffirmed his grip and suddenly the wrist pressing into the front of my neck became like an iron bar. Breathing had always been out of the question, but now an intense pressure built behind my eyes. I had slipped to the ground, my chest was being pressed into the tarmac. I saw small distant stars moving slowly over the surface of the pavement only inches from my face. People were walking past. The whole thing had taken only six seconds. I passed out.

When I rejoined the uncivilised world I didn't know how much later it was. I found myself sprawled in a chair, looking down at my legs splayed on the floor. Yes, I was wearing the same clothes. I raised my head; that was a sore and wobbly operation. I was in an office. My wallet was on top of a cabinet in front of me. When Tony opened the door and rushed in I could see I was in the bicycle shop. I was in the boarded-off section at the back. Through the open door I could see the bicycles and beyond them through the glass window I could see the street moving past. It was busier now, picking up from the pace of the early morning. I felt like I'd been dragged sideways out of time.

Tony was carrying a bucket of water and a flannel. He looked wild. When he saw that I'd come round he said:

'Thank God!'

He uttered a gasp, half-way to a laugh. I wished he would move more slowly. I held up my hand, ready to give an apology, but nothing came out. My throat was bruised and I was giddy. My head rolled on my shoulders. I remember thinking, 'I'm not yet in control', and strangely it was a relief to know that.

Tony splashed the flannel into the water. I was dreading that he was going to put it on my face. Through the open door I could see his mate with the front wheel of my bicycle between his knees. He gave the handlebars several harsh jerks, and with an absurd squeaking they were slowly straightened back into the proper position. The carrier looked broken. All these things were very new and disconcerting. It was as though I'd been born again. Tony pressed the flannel against my forehead. Damn. He asked:

'Are you all right?'

'Yes . . . I'll be fine in a minute. I just need to . . .'

I felt happy. I'd gone backwards. Another Incident, a medium to horrible Incident, yes, but I was having thoughts like these: 'Saved! I've been saved by something, something

120

soothing . . . a backwash of failure. Back again . . . resting, with just the oily sentimental fear in my stomach. Nothing complicated, nothing difficult. Surely there's no room for vanity now. Square one. I won't have to do a thing . . .' The Test was advancing into the distance.

I didn't want to know what had happened. The Item had jumped me from behind. Better to know nothing, just shrug it off, forget it, like tripping and falling over. A curse, and then carry on. Ha! If there's one thing the Original Incident has taught me, it's that I won't forget. I will be allowed to do nothing else but remember, but I'm used to that now, that's home, and it's safe. Tony asked:

'How d'you feel?'

'All right. Nothing serious. I just need to sit down for a while longer.'

'Try it with your head between your knees.'

'I might be sick.'

'No, try it. It'll be better like that.'

Tony put one hand on the front of my head and one hand on the back. Obligingly I let him tilt my head down between my knees.

'Thank God you're all right . . . Thank God. I didn't know . . .'

My stomach contracted, and the contents were thrown out onto the floor. The taste was the worst thing. Tony moved quickly, but still gallantly kept hold of my head. His voice was agitated, full of difficulties:

'I'm really sorry . . .'

He dashed away to get the bucket. He always moves so quickly. I didn't feel comfortable, but it's true that I was less giddy. 'I'll be all right,' I assured him. I wanted to thank him, if

121

only he'd stop moving. He was putting my wallet back in my pocket for me. He said:

'I didn't know, you see. I thought you were making off with one of our bikes.'

Chrissy left me. It was a little time ago now that I got the message. I found it when I came home from work, written in a notebook, and then torn out and put in that traditional place we all know about, the famous mantelpiece. There's no beginning to the letter. It starts straight off the blocks and doesn't stop until the end.

I am going to write this letter to you because you ought to know how I feel EXACTLY at this moment. I've been packing up my things all day and I realised after I finished that there is nothing left, i.e. you have put nothing into this place, not a single possession that you've put around you to make this 'home'. This made me suddenly very depressed. When I came into this flat one and a half years ago I thought it was empty, but only because you hadn't bothered. Now when I'm leaving I know that it's you! You are empty. I am leaving nothing but emptiness behind. There was nothing there. I can hardly picture you in my mind's eye any more, you've turned into a shadow and it all seems such a waste of fucking time, the hours I've spent trying to coax you into some real hot-blooded form of life. You've evaporated from in front of my eyes like a conjuring trick; I might as well have been

trying to have sex with a bloody hologram. Above everything I keep on thinking what a waste of time. What did
you want from me? I can't work it out – please help.
When we had the row you talked like a sociology book,
with men are like this and women are like that, and
women want that more than men though don't they? But
where are you, YOU? Hiding behind something, some
neutral plastic mask of masculinity? I don't suppose
you'll answer this letter. I am trying to salvage something
from the year and a half because otherwise I'll never ever
feel like giving my time to anyone ever again, and I don't
want to get that hopelessly bitter. It's not that I can't
remember good times. D'you remember being in the car
trying to avoid Mr Popupandseeme, making love on top
of the hill, and getting lost on the way back? But even in
those days the time we spent together just floated past us,
the existing minute only. That's the only place you live,
the existing minute. When I think of the row I hate you. I
know my suspicions are correct but I'm frightened of the
knowledge, so I chose to believe you. But I know you
fully intended to tell me. I didn't force it out of you. The
reason for the summer was balls, and the rest of it after
the summer; we pretended we were just settling down
through a few misunderstandings. You were avoiding
me, and that's how it came out. Sex is always a manifes-
tation. I can't believe that in this tiny flat we've been
living so far apart. When I look back on it the row was a
sick game that you played all right. You stood by the
window knowing that if you stood there long enough I
would have to ask you what's wrong. I remember clearly
the way you said 'nothing'. It's like a sitcom that I have

been forced to take *seriously*. It is torture. Please, please, write to me and admit you are wrong and say sorry. DON'T HIDE!! After you forced me to force you to have a row, you just announce it, like you might tell me you're going to take a day off work. It sounded like a legal delivery, a series of injunctions to prevent me from ever being free enough to love you. 'During the summer I had an affair with someone else.' GOD! I've never had to suffer such BORING cruelty. And then all your theories about 'men this' and 'women that' making me feel like a frog that's had its legs pulled off by YOU. What did you do afterwards, go straight away and scoff all the cakes and jelly? When I saw your clothes in the cupboard I could easily have torn the lot of them to shreds and thrown them out of the window. I want you to know that you're lucky I didn't. What was that summer away all about? Why did you come back at all if you thought you'd made a mistake with me? I gave you everything you said you needed. I agreed to walk down to the tube by myself. You told me you wanted to be 'still and quiet' at night so it's me that's wasted my time and my body on your lies. What is the truth? Why didn't you tell the truth from the outset so I wouldn't be sitting here feeling so frustrated at this time I've wasted on your lies? Did you know what you were doing? WHO ARE YOU? I'm scared shitless of never being able to trust myself with anyone ever again. I have run out of hope. I look forward to the future and I see nothing, nothing but myself, struggling alone to put food in my mouth and nothing more. I honestly think I might be unable to laugh. Wherever that comes from has been blocked up, dried out. I feel like a wasted human being. There is a lack of any potential in the future, and the past has been pulled from under my feet. I am writing this letter to let you know that I think you are SHIT. Please have the decency to reply to me, because I need to know things to help me start again. I'm not interested in a stupid note, I want a reply. Please learn to be honest. I will know what I think when I know what you think. Is there anything you've got from living with me? I've got to go now.

There is an instruction that exists at the back of my head. I don't know where it comes from but I'm making repeated use of it: 'Don't stop!' I say it out loud with manic cheerfulness. If you allow yourself to stop, the emptiness of the room closes in to haunt you. The pictures are no longer like old friends there to reassure you and advise you that yes, you are the same person you once were. Now they are like ghosts of a past moment, capable only of reminding you when and where you bought them, not of anything since.

I can't deny that my flat is gloomy. It is more than empty with Chrissy gone. It's damaged.

I'm not going to move. I am not suffering any extra torment by remaining in the flat. I am not reminded every day of her changing moods. The flat now only has one mood, one air, that speaks to me of what? Nothing as solid as a statement, more of a request. The flat is asking me to rip it out, to change its guts, move her stuff out of the lounge, mainly. I don't know how she's going to get this furniture back. Perhaps it's meant to represent some sort of hope ... a hint maybe ...? I've already moved the bed to the opposite corner. The flat requests surgery to recover from the damage she did to it. I open the windows a lot.

126

Small resentments pester me. Why should I suddenly have to eat off the bare table instead of the cloth? My handful of records stand useless because she's taken the stereo. I have no change of sheets, so I have to pick up my bag from the launderette on the same day.

One of the first instructions on my list is 'clean up'. This is because corners have been revealed for the first time in a year and the dirt has found refuge, gathering in the exact shape that avoids the cleaning process. For example, the two triangles of dust and debris behind the speakers. I wonder to what extent dust is made up of human skin. I find myself thinking in that way, like a Sunday magazine. The magazines are the only company I keep. If only I was allowed to relax, alone with a bit of food, like the rabbits.

'Don't stop!'

Did Chrissy behave unfairly? No. Did I? No. She had no idea of my reality, and I have no idea about hers. We're cut out of different magazines. The reality is simple and cruel and as constant as the air of the flat. It is inescapable. You have to breathe it constantly. That's what you have to do to maintain a successful relationship. You can't change the facts when they rub against you. Chrissy couldn't stand it and left. It's melodrama. I am cast as the villain. I am only the villain to her, to no one else. As for me, I have my own villain.

'Don't stop!'

I reach for the phone and dial Tony.

'Tony!'

'Hello.'

'You game?'

'Yup. Pick you up?'

'D'you mind?'

'No, easy. Half six all right?'

A savage reprimand to myself, to be so self-pitying and lonely as to think of myself as being cut out from a magazine.

I have been renewing my relationship with a few old sounds which I had forgotten about. The bathroom tap drip has a rhythm which is impossible to follow, however many times you try. Hours of pleasure are available from the thankless task of trying to identify one particular sound that comes through from the flat upstairs. It could be a bead curtain. It could be a handful of enraged locusts shut in a biscuit tin. No, out of the question. The noise happens in short bursts every now and again. Perhaps it's an executive toy.

I go to the bathroom before getting changed. As I pass the bath I give a small cheer. It's a moment of triumph for my blue sponge, shaped now like a more significant, silent hippopotamus. Once again it is enthroned, the only thing sitting on the tiles behind the bath. I haven't looked at myself in the mirror so much for ages.

I examine myself closely for signs of wear. I am in extreme close-up in the mirror. You're as old as your body, there's no getting away from that one. For no reason tears are welling up in my eyes. I continue to stare. I try not to blink. When they've been burning in my eyes for some time I find a reason for them. Cruelty has invaded the flat! Unseen, unknown, it has found its way in on the bottom of people's shoes. It's an accumulative poison, and it's been lurking in the corners, feeding off the fragments of human skin, waiting for an opportunity to present itself.

I stand by the front door, looking at the spyhole, and then at my Opponent. She is waiting there, one hand tensed on the latch, standing with one leg broken at the knee, like a decrepit servant waiting for the signal. If I take so much as a half-step towards her she'll open the door for me.

I feel angry. Why should I encourage myself in all this? I think, 'Anger. Good. Good for training.'

In the bedroom the dressing-table has been closed down. It's no longer a going concern. The wardrobe doors shut properly. I change into my jock-strap and remove the ring from my third finger. I think of the words of cheap songs – that one about the bed being too big and the frying-pan too wide. I would like to get an even bigger bed, a massive piece of furniture with curtains round it, and a frying-pan to match. I'm angry with the bedroom. A cheap square block of a room with a boarded-up fire-place and a thin hard carpet. This room was derelict the moment it was built. All the blocks of flats stand their ground outside the window. Time and the weather are wreaking a quick and merciless revenge on the character-less stumps.

I pack my small bag and for once I remember shampoo. I've asked to borrow shampoo an embarrassing number of times. I'm ready. As usual there is the slight anxiousness, not un-pleasant. Tony is late, so I am stuck with nothing to do. Looking out of the window, I remind myself, 'Chrissy is out there somewhere. Perhaps at this very moment she is reading my reply.' It's a huge city spread out beneath me. I'm senti-mentally attracted to think of the fate of one struggling indi-vidual somewhere out there. The rush hour is over; she will be home, wherever 'home' is for her. I can persuade myself that I'm in a Walt Disney film. I will have to go out and find her, using a network of underground friends who all work at strange jobs during the night – bakers, cleaners, dairymen, newspaper delivery boys. The doorbell sounds.

Tony drives a Triumph Stag but it doesn't have the V8 engine. This is typical of Tony. He aims for the mark, but always strikes a little bit wide one way or another. Even so, the car is a good ride. It turns the heads of strangers and they hate you for having it. You have to be careful looking out of the side window at traffic lights. There is a limitless capacity for meaningful animosity, such as: an Item comes up and punches the window. 'Hey! That's my car. C'mon. Gimme my car!' He continues to punch the window. He looks furious, as though it really is his car and we've just stolen it. Maybe he's persuaded himself of that, some way or other. Tony takes off even though the lights are on red. There's hooting coming at us from all directions, and Tony is forced to take a left turn. I notice that on his lap a personal defence canister of CS gas has miraculously appeared.

Tony is always friendly to me now. He has a long-term guilt problem about nearly killing me that time with his beginner's enthusiasm for the strangle. He thought I was stealing one of his bikes, of all things. It's difficult to know if he'll ever be a friend. For now he's passable company and a convenient chauffeur on Tuesdays, Thursdays and Saturdays. I ask:

'Have you seen Chrissy?'

'Er . . . yes. Once.'

'So she's still living in the area, then?'

'I don't know. She was on her way back from work. I just saw her pass by.'

'Did you have words, at all?'

'Oh, just the usual.'

'Did she say she was all right?'

'She seemed all right, considering.'

'When was it you saw her?'

'This was . . . last week.'

Chrissy wouldn't have got the reply by then. It was quite long; I took my time over it. I look at Tony and think, 'You four-eyed bastard. You've been talking about me behind my back.' My next question I have to take my time to build up to, because, at the same time as being a question, it's something else, something that gives a sensual shifting very similar to the one experienced when you're having a shit; isn't it like that, when you're seen to be making a confession?

'Did she mention anything about me, at all?' (Sudden anal relief.)

'Not much. She said she was sad, you know, and that she'd tried hard but couldn't make it work.'

We continue in the car, speaking no more. Occasionally I indulge in my new-found taste for inventing insults suitable for various innocent pedestrians. A tousle-haired youth dreaming about girls gets 'Bog Head'. An Oriental trotting across the road on his way home to his family gets 'Get out of it, you box-faced wog.' A well-built woman on her way to the pub gets 'Jelly waps'. All insults are uttered with maximum sneer and volume from the safety of the enclosed car.

I am looking out for Chrissy, of course. She is amongst this litter of human beings somewhere.

In the car-park Tony likes to pull in next to the two rich cars. I still haven't found out, after all this time, who rides in either of those two cars. Inside we pay our money at the hatch. I hear the familiar smack of a throw being broken on the mat.

After judo I will go home and the London smog won't seem

half as heavy on my head. I can throw it off. I will eat a carefully prepared fillet of fish stolen from work, and, having told myself enough times to stop holding my breath, I will sleep soundly. Somewhere, maybe, Chrissy will be taking another man on a small makeshift bed, or in the lounge of some other maisonette belonging to a friend of hers.

'Alone . . . ' 'Lonely . . . ' 'On your own . . . ' Such mournful expressions.

I am in front of a panel of judges. I don't know who the judges are – that isn't important. All I know is that they've started the competition, and it's they alone who decide which one of us will be the winner.

This is my own personal interview. I must state my case now because this is the only chance we get. There is no appeal, no long-winded deliberation. I'm tense because the judges are going to be so emotional. I can't see their faces properly. This is how it should be. They don't speak, but I know they've asked me a question:

'What makes you think that you have maintained an erection for a longer duration of time than any of the other contestants?'

'It's because of the building,' I reply.

The girl is down between the wall and the chairs that are evenly spaced round the boardroom table. She is lying all crumpled like a bird that's been shot down in flight. I go down myself; it's like I'm landing. She turns round to look at me, lifting her face from the carpet so that it twists above the line of her neck. I don't know who she is, but we're in this together. Her hands come back towards me and start to pull the black dress up round her waist. Her head drops back down; she has seen my erection. We work at each other round the table. I can see that the oscillation of her breast is geared like a machine to the plugging action of my erection. She is grinning, secretly.

132

The judges have asked me, 'Why the building? What is it about a building that gives you an erection?'

I don't know if the judges are there or not. I'm standing looking out of a window. It's an office window. I'm looking down on a curved façade of Georgian town houses. The white pillars gleam in the sunlight; the whole frontage is in a perfect, graceful condition. It's pleasant to stand there and have an erection for as long as I like. My erection is straining. It's bigger than it's ever been.

I feel a tremendous relief. There's no worry about anything. I'm simply standing at a window looking out onto a peaceful, sunlit street, idly stroking an erection that'll stay there for as long as I do. The wet street reflects the sun.

I still haven't come yet. The girl is digging her nails in and pulling at me. Her legs are gaping beautifully. One or two chairs have been knocked over. Her chin rakes from side to side. Still I haven't come. This might be a good thing.

The judges ask, 'Who is this girl?'

I reply, 'I don't know.'

While I'm looking closely at the strap of the girl's suspender marking her flesh I realise that I know something. I ought to tell the judges.

'I don't know her name but she's something to do with Toots.'

'Something?'

'Maybe she was his girlfriend once. I don't know for sure.'

The suspender slackens and shifts with the girl's legs. She is turning over. Her fanny opens rudely because she's dipping her back, so I carry on working. I can see everything very clearly.

'Why the building?' ask the judges. I am not ashamed to be stroking my erection. The Georgian façade looks familiar in the wet sunlight; at any minute a rainbow might appear. This is important.

'Because that's where it happened. It was in a room . . .'

133

'What sort of room?'

'A boardroom. In that building. The sight of it is enough to give me an erection for as long as I want.'

'Exactly where in the building?' ask the judges.

'There ...' I point out a doorway. The pillars are dirty and weathered by the acid city grime. The steps are broken. The doorstep is scrappy with litter; the bits of paper are soggy and inert from lying there such an age.

The girl is trying harder to make me come because she's tired and drying out. I wish she'd stop trying so hard. I want her to be completely inert. I should have asked her to play dead. It's too late now.

The judges are unanimous. I've won.

March 24

There are several Items at judo. This, after all, is what my Opponent demanded, but I can't deal with it very well. I'm either stupidly friendly or self-consciously aloof. On the mat I try hard to beat them, or give it all away in the name of training.

There is one particular Item. He's not a perfect specimen, because he's overweight, but (sickening surprise) he has got the camelhair overcoat. He can only wrap his black belt once round his middle. Some people call him 'Toots'. What happens when you have to try and get to grips with someone who's not far off being a good imitation of a listed building? I found out.

Despite the difference in our weight and grade, I am facing Toots in a three-minute bout. My consolation is that he is

134

expected to help me, not break me. We are only training. When we bow I see his belly dip; then we step forward. He makes no effort to find a grip. He's not even looking for it, or worrying about my hand coming in. When I come into contact with his collar I get the message. I can feel everything in the first few seconds of gripping up. This is why he isn't making any fuss. The man is a twenty-stone human gate-post. It's no surprise that he hasn't tried to strike my hand away, or get a grip before mine. He just stands there, and allows me all the time I need to get my right hand in close to his neck and my left tight on his elbow. When I'm done he puts his hands up and holds my hips. This is new to me. He can stop me coming in for a reverse throw, but I wouldn't think of taking that weight onto my back. I could go in for a reverse and then collapse one knee, and hope to get deep enough under him to make him fall over his own weight. If he is holding my hips, that is what he is afraid of. It is not an offensive stance. I could try a sweep. With a big snap of a movement I pull him towards me to try and get his weight moving, so I can knock the moving foot from under him. The snap has no effect. He simply doesn't move. Some people train to become so rock solid that you can't trick them into anything. This man has taken root in the mat. He has never looked in my eyes at all. He is concentrating on doing something with my body. He looks at it in an every-day sort of way, as though it's a box or a sack. His bottom lip hangs pendulous, with short breaths passing over it. He gives a great shout and does a straight lift. I'm in the air suspended by my hips. My trousers are cutting into my crack. The only hope is to go for a standing strangle, so I dive in on his neck. He falls forward, and we land with a crash. His weight has expelled the wind from my body. I am incapable. He's still resting all the weight of his stomach on my chest. I will not be able to breathe until he gets off. My hands are trapped. I can't even submit. When he start swivelling round it's like being drilled by a giant boulder, which finally comes to rest on my face. One of my eyes is closed against his belly; with the other I can see the mesh of pubic hair tracking down from his sunken whirlpool of a stomach button. I cannot imagine him swinging from an umbilical cord. It would have to be made out of hemp. He swivels again, and sits on my chest. At last one of my hands is free to slap the mat. I submit. As Toots lifts his weight a loud fart breaks onto my chest. The warmth of it is obscene. People are laughing while I try and get some air.

'Toots is called Toots,' says Tony later, 'because Dave Lee once said that it was like trying to have a fight with a motor car. Toots heard about it and took to saying "Toot toot" whenever he was sitting on someone.'

'So now he calls himself Toots.'

'It stuck. He doesn't do it any more though. Now he just farts on people.'

'Nice man.'

'No. Not nice. But he's funny.'

I can see him undressing on the other side of the changing-room. Strong male bodies criss-cross through the mist in front of me, heading for the showers, while behind them Toots sits unashamed. If it's all right for everyone to be seen naked, it's all right for Toots to scratch his balls and examine the inside of his foreskin. His great belly hangs out like an overnight bag. His upper body is strong, and the black skin is oiled, I think. His mouth always hangs a bit slack, an open drain into the stomach. His face is deadpan. I return to watch his face every time; looking anywhere else is a trick to make it seem like I'm

136

not taking an interest. He is saying something to the man next to him. Three people are laughing now, but he continues speaking through the laughter as though it didn't exist.

I think, 'He is only able to *be* like that because he is *shaped* like that.'

It's when he has finally changed, and put on the camelhair overcoat, that I feel the usual twinge. He strides out treading heavily through the heels of his shoes. He is an Item. There are many other Items here, but he's the one that breaks the bag.

April 2

The spring air is still sharp at night sometimes, but summer is on the way. There's a different brand of darkness now – it's thinner. I was walking through it the night I found the coat, and it's easier, but I still try to think of anything that will make it safe. My exclusion zone is a pathetic defence; it is really only a heightened surveillance. It's not even as good as infra-red. I saw the coat as part of an answer.

So I am walking home late from work, striding hard towards my empty flat. The popular tune is under my breath: trala dee da. I want to be thinking of something else except the fact that I am having to enforce the Exclusion Zone, so, as quite often, it's the 'perhaps Chrissy is waiting for me in my flat' game. She's kept the key, after all. Ba pa boowa. It's possible she's waiting. She would be nervous, standing in the middle of the room. I hang onto her phrases as light entertainment while my feet still have to carry me through the roofless corridors of streets. She would say, 'I hope you don't mind, I still have the key, I'll give it back if you want . . . dee dum deeda . . .' 'I don't mind,' I say. 'D'you want some tea . . .?' 'All right.' I can see her legs, her brown hair shining, the crooked tilt of her mouth. The act of remembering the same things . . . I latch onto her. It's like I am cocking my leg even on the memory. It's unpleasant knowing she's not going to be there. Dee dum dee . . . daaa . . . 'What's that?' she would ask, pointing at my find. 'It's a coat. I found it in a skip,' I reply. 'It looks like it . . . ' She would try a laugh.

The coat is tatty, but it's a leather-backed donkey jacket. They don't make them any more. I have rescued it from a skip, under cover of darkness this very night, and now it's over my shoulder, sitting like a large dead cat, smelling of building dust.

Chrissy would pick it up, gingerly, in mock horror. 'Looks like it needs the kiss of life,' she'd say. What about me?

My reply is urgent: 'Kiss me' . . . Dood'n doo . . . 'Help me.' . . . Waa . . .

In the kitchen I would operate the tea-making process mechanically. 'I'm a vegetarian now.' She's surprised: 'Are you . . .' 'I've changed jobs. A vegetarian place. Serves fish as well. It's OK. The walk back is *hell* . . .' We would stand together in the kitchen. We might as well be a couple of guests at someone else's wedding. There would be a vast knowledge in the kitchen. It's inarticulate. It occupies every single inch of space except what's cut out by the shape of our bodies. I would have forgotten to press the switch on the kettle, of course. Chrissy and I would have to start again, laboriously.

I'm progressing slowly, that's something to hang onto. The pavement is disappearing behind me.

I sing under my breath on the way home like a sordid Mary Poppins without any words.

I have accepted a severe reduction in wages by taking my new job at the vegetarian restaurant. It's a high-class establishment that doesn't make much money. The hours are more or less the same. I'm either on the early shift, from ten in the morning to four in the afternoon, or on the late shift, from four until whenever, or both. I try to keep Tuesday and Thursday evenings and Saturday afternoons free for judo. The customers are friendly and they like to talk about food, which is a change. Of course I have brought my own set of Items with me. They stand in their block of wood in a new home, and they aren't used for meat at all, only fish. It's a commonplace event, a small step for the vegetarian cause: the disarming of one chef.

I am less able to know what I think. Chrissy would be glad to know that my theories are awash. This is because I'm at the fulcrum of an idea that once went one way, but now I've seen the possibility of the whole argument tilting in the other direction. Here I am, a dreary speck sitting in an empty dusty flat. I've collected a number of experiences. I have been treated by the world in this way, so I am like this. Now if I turn myself around and look the other way, I can see the argument lurching uncontrollably. Is my character the very thing that's caused me to turn the experience into a predicament? I am like I am, so the world treats me just so. The shape of my character is now an unknown quantity. If I was switched into my predicament by the Original Incident, then that's easy. I cannot blame myself for being an automatic man. But if I seized on the Incident in order to cause my own predicament, that makes me well on the way towards automasochism. My head swims when I think of the possibility of my being responsible for everything that happens to me.

'Don't stop!'

I pick up the leather-backed donkey jacket and a large pair of scissors. While I'm working I can enjoy myself pondering over past scenes of humiliation. One of them requires me to focus on the occasion of my seeing Chrissy for the second time. It was quite by fluke, and in the place which gave me the idea of how to help her, or trap her, or trick her, or however else she would now define my behaviour.

Of course I don't know her name yet. All I know is that it's the same girl that I saw sitting on the kerb outside the Screaming Maisonette. I had torn up the note after she'd disappeared from the eye of my window. Now, two weeks later, I'm looking at the back of her head as she stands in the queue, three places ahead of me. It gives me a start to see her. It's like when you have a word that you've never seen before. Suddenly it starts to appear, maybe three or four times. This girl is becoming like magic.

She steps forward to the rent officer whose face moves in and out of a small square of wire mesh set in chipboard. I can hear her business. She says:

'I wanted to know if you had any places going.'

'I'm sorry, not at the moment.'

'But I've looked round. There's loads of empty flats boarded up.'

'I'm sorry, Miss, but I can't just give them to you, just like that. They're all about to be renovated, those lot.'

'What about if I renovate it myself?'

'That's not the point. You have to join the list. Some people have been asking ahead of you, you know.'

'How do I join this list?'

'Go and see the Council.'

'How long will it take?'

140

'Have you got a baby?'

'Not on me, no.'

'Well all I know is that some people with kids have been waiting for years.'

'Thank you, that's fine.'

'Right you are.'

'I'll be all right in the bus station for another couple of years. It's quite comfortable.'

'There's no need to be like that, young lady. It's none of my fault. It's the Council. If there was a decent politician in the whole world . . .'

'Forget it. Sorry.'

The girl turns away and walks out, avoiding all the pairs of eyes queued up behind her. Each pair has the thought behind them that she might go and steal their flats. They'd better hurry indoors and lock themselves in. I'm conscious of the big coloured rent book in my hands. Everyone else in the queue has a rent book. They are orange flags put out by the queue to wave her off, hideous dayglo warnings, like at the scene of an accident.

I turn out of the queue and follow her. I can feel the eyes burning my back with their opinion of me as a really obvious young prick. I can see her back as she swings round the corner of the rent office towards the exit from the estate. My spare bedroom is empty. I've wanted a tenant for some time. I look at the line of her legs as they hit against the skirt. She is walking fast, aggressively. All I need is a shout, that initial shout, then I'll be forced into doing the rest. Please, give me a shout! Why can't I do it? There is no shout, nothing but breath in my throat. Then, as I stop, I direct an asphyxiated half-squawk of annoyance at my feet as I twist them into the pavement, turning to kick the fence. For God's sake! My feet are free to run and catch her up. My voice is free to ask her. I'm standing here under a grey sky, with my arms free, my legs free, but my heart and my mind are locked, jammed in some ridiculous . . . crash! This is the result of my silent accident with fear. Crash! I kick the fence again.

I watch her as she walks past the Alley. She is escaping me. She wasn't even aware of it, but that was my first attempt to seduce her. She is out of sight round the corner now. If you boil it down to the bare bones, I've just tried to take her clothes off. The dark gob of the Alley condemns me as pathetic.

I turn into the estate again. All the little trees they planted have been taken and used as war toys. I've lost my place in the queue. I wish that was a good metaphor, but it's easy to rejoin the queue, and I still have my orange flag. I hate the queue with its fatuous 'good morning' style of conversation, interspersed with the odd statement on human life. The face behind the grille is friendly when you're up to date. 'Good morning!' he says. I reply, 'No.'

The leather-backed donkey jacket is progressing well. It's a good thing to fill in the time. The minutes pass by so laboriously now, I'm waiting for the end of each one. The bottom third of the donkey jacket lies on the floor at my feet. It had been far too long; I'd looked like a drowned bird the first time I put it on. It's been worth ruining the scissors – the difference is dramatic. The jacket stops at my hips. No longer do I look like a bottle of brown ale. The bottom hem swings too wide, of course, but I know what I need to do. I go in search of the leather strap and the rivet gun and a hammer.

I think often of Toots standing in his well-worn judo suit

and black belt, positioning himself, knees bent, as solid as a church on the mat. It's beyond me how you get to beat a man like that. The next step in defence is obvious; I must not fall for the trap he set me. He wanted me to grip up first so he had his hands free to grab for my hips once he was in there. If I had tried to plant my weight further back at that stage he simply would have leaned on me until I fell flat on my face. The only thing to do is to try and trap his hands from the very beginning. At least it might take him a bit longer to beat me. Of course it's not something I have to worry about particularly. He is not in my weight category, and he's way ahead of my grade. I will never come up against him in a competition or a grading. No one will expect me to beat him in training unless he allows me to. Why bother working out a plan of attack? Marekh, for example, with his leaping defence of *hairogoshi*, is much more my sort of challenge. Ah, but I'm not allowed to behave myself. My Opponent holds her hands out wide and herds me into it. It is, after all, one of her Tests in its most obvious form. Toots is a jumbo Item. He is almost two Items rolled into one. He stands on the mat as impregnable as the Test itself. I'm stuck in front of him, anchored by her waving, rheumatic arms. Unknown to her I have a plan. She thinks this training is for her amusement, but when I've done enough, I'm going to turn and use it against her. I'm going to throw her over the balcony.

With the donkey jacket laid out on the table I apply the rivet gun to the holes in the leather strap, securing it to the bottom hem of the jacket. It's beginning to come together. The patches of leather on the shoulders need gluing down. They've been torn to shreds by the work the jacket's done. What did the owner carry on his shoulders before he threw it in the skip? I would guess bricks or plaster. He must have been a very big man.

With the leather glued down and the strap riveted onto the bottom edge it begins to look the part. The jacket is mended, but it still looks roughty-toughty.

For how much longer am I going to have to endure the binding of this tight aggression and hatred, this mad old lady who's suddenly come to stay? It's been difficult trying to hide her. She is tedious. I have to lock her away up here. Nobody must know. If you let your eye off her she's likely to pick up a poker from the fire and gouge out somebody's eye. She offers a permanent threat of embarrassment. She doesn't really understand anything; she has one opinion, and that's all. Her opinion is constantly being confirmed, of course. Therefore, although she is senile and emotional, her hysteria is always predictable. She's like a dreadful gland that's suddenly been activated.

The buckle is not fitted to the leather strap, and I am punching holes in the other end with the hammer and nail. There are two tucks in the material at the front of the jacket to make the broad swathe of leather gather it in correctly to the hips. The collar needs cutting down to size.

I imagine Toots facing the age-bitten old Opponent on the judo mat. The referee calls them together to take the bow. Toots takes it from the waist in the proper manner. The Opponent just stands there, moving from one foot to another, her wispy hair pointing in all directions. Clearly she doesn't know the rules. Toots steps forward and plants himself in the usual pose – knees bent, arms at the ready. My old lady cocks an eye at him, then rushes, but stops almost immediately. She backs away, circling round behind him. He turns with her.

144

'I hate you!' she screams, her face rising in colour. Toots is put off by the unorthodox approach. He decides to wait and see what happens. She runs in a small circle around him, stopping every now and again to hurl the words again. Toots is going to appeal to the referee. He points to her, and, with his face deadpan as usual, says, 'She's cheating.'

The referee takes my old lady to one side. She is shaking as he takes hold of her arm and advises her on the proper behaviour. The referee very kindly helps her to tie her dressing-gown belt which has fallen undone. No one wants to see her slip; it's embarrassing. She never once looks at the referee. She's staring at Toots.

When the fight starts again she stays put, rocking slightly on her feet. Toots approaches. She is just standing there, transfixed like a rabbit. He comes a bit closer. She puts her hands in her pockets, drawing the dressing-gown tight by pressing into them. Toots walks forward and prepares to grip up. As usual he doesn't appear to be concentrating. I wonder if he's noticed that her face is starting to spasm as though there were insects crawling about on the inside of her mouth. All her hair is pointing at Toots. Very gently he walks forward and takes hold of her dressing-gown collar. She, the mad old wreck, takes a gun out of her pocket and shoots him dead.

Fortunately the heavy felt cloth of the jacket doesn't fray when you cut it. I am happy with the line of glue smeared into the edge to hold it together. I am not, after all, requiring a delicate finish.

I've had an idea from looking at the Dali painting. Say that when Toots has been carried off and everyone's gone home after the drama of the shooting, I'm still waiting. I have to be sure no one is watching. When I've checked all the other rooms and switched off the lights I go into the women's changing-room. I kneel next to the Opponent and take off my belt. With a last look round to see that no one is observing me at this very private ritual, I open the drawer in my stomach. It slides out quite easily if you pull it smoothly and evenly on both sides. I take care not to rip her floppy skin as I bundle her inside. I have to hurry or someone might see. It's because I have to hide her.

While I'm working away at the coat it's pleasant to indulge in imagining these scenes. It's necessary to take measures when you've only got your own jacket for company. The collar is perfect now. It stands up in an even two-inch curve round my neck. Two buttons need replacing, but that can wait.

It weighs heavy in my hand, and the leather belt at the bottom hangs convincingly. I sling it over the back of the chair and look at it critically. The rivets are disappointing. They were a good idea, but they look wrong. They shine too cheaply. I hope that they'll go dull with rust after a while.

When I shrug the jacket onto my back the smell of the building dust catches me. The weight of it is reassuring on my shoulders. There comes the immediate sensation of good health that accompanies clothes that you think you need. The belt dangles effectively. My shoulders are bulky. The scarred surface of the leather testifies to many hard hours of work. These broad shoulders have lifted hods full of bricks, and broken down doors, and cleared a path through many a crowded pub. My own shoulders are slipstreaming underneath. When I buckle up the belt it sits on my hips and I look like I might be able to drag a lorry weighing several metric tonnes with my teeth or pull a wheelie on any size of motorbike, or fly a plane and land it on a short grass runway in the

146

Andes mountains. I could stop the running mugger with one crunch of my fist, and I can break up an argument now. I can distil my revenge and chase it with a one-track mind. I can ride the last tube train home.

Seven

August 18

Toots, that big fat bastard! The man has the knack of making money. Some of it is lining my pocket, I'm glad to say.

On my first night he sat next to me in his glitzy robes and said:

'It's like my family here. They pay to come and be my family.'

When Toots speaks he throws it out to the whole room. There was nobody there, but still he spread himself around as though he had to contact an audience who were ready for his every word. He didn't look at me, even though I was the only other human in the room.

The nightclub is divided into three. My kitchen is in the middle, as small as a cupboard between the bar and the stage. At each end of this crammed-in utility room there's a swing-door which allows a fierce slice of kitchen-light to escape into the gloom where the punters are spending their money drinking or watching a show or dancing. Not many are investing in food.

Through one set of doors is the bar, which is done out in black and red, with lights well under control in the corners. The quietness of the room has been built in with sound-proofed walls. There is always the expectation of something sinister going on in the bar. The black seats look too full; they're soft and fertile for underhand opportunity.

The other side of my hutch opens out onto the stage, which has been built like a mini amphitheatre. You have to charge the doors quite hard with your hip, and that lets you out onto the topmost level, from where stairs descend through three levels to the stage itself. Toots' 'family' dance on the stage with a video screen behind them, or sprawl in groups round the tables sprouting empty beer bottles, watching the cabaret. There are erotic dancers, lunatic comedians, political satirists, kick-boxers and wrestlers, and Toots himself, every now and again, getting up to speak to his hundreds of relations.

On that first night Toots was waiting, his lower lip slack, pendulous. Soon the doors would open, and his family would come to pay him. He was swaying gently in his seat, looking like a fly-catcher. I said:

'We need to talk about the menu.'

'What's wrong with it?' he asked the empty room.

'We need to change it every week. Make it more interesting.'

'People don't come here to eat.'

At that I asked myself what I was doing here. What was he up to, paying someone like me all this money if there was never any idea of getting the family sitting together with their jaws wrapped round some good food?

'Perhaps they will if we put a decent menu out.'

'I leave it to you. You do as you want. All I want is Spinach Flan, or Aubergine with Crab. About eleven. Each night.'

The last two phrases came in between a couple of hard sucks of breath. Was he nervous? I'm sure he cultivates the idea that he's unfathomable. Despite myself I grew big on that line of

149

his: 'I leave it to you.' Every now and again he says something which makes my heart strike a little harder. Yes, there is a new life around me here, which I may or may not be able to take up and use as my own.

The doors open at nine and there's usually one or two of the hardline regulars hanging about waiting. At that point I disappear to the kitchen to set the Boy to work. This isn't easy. He is a lounger, always trying to rest as many parts of his body as possible against the metal surfaces and the wall. His apron is unwashed and undone, on purpose. He looks patchy, as though he's been boiled. He's been eyeing me with his practised weird look, ever since I started. The reason, as I thought then? He wanted to make me think he was special, and he was frightened that, since I'd been asked in over his head, I might be special instead.

'How much is Toots paying you?' he asked, early on, confident of his insolence. When I told him he lifted his chin and laughed, with his eyes squeezed, but still looking at me steadily. I asked:

'What's the matter with that?'

'Nothing's the matter.'

'Why is it funny?'

'Oh it's not funny,' he replied, 'It's a serious amount of money. Very serious.'

He shook his head. I thought at the time that perhaps he was making a habit of mocking me because he was friendly with the last chef. I carried on with giving him an order:

'Fire up the coals.'

'Already?'

'We're open for business, aren't we?'

'No one ever comes 'til ten thirty.'

'Someone might.'

He made a reluctant turn and reached for the gas-tap.

Toots invited me here ... that was a surprise. I didn't see what was coming, but I got as far as marking the surprise. He had taken to trashing me after training, in a friendly way; I was just one of those people suitable for his short abrupt comments when I was a new boy at the sport. He learnt that I was a chef, I don't know how – I didn't tell him. I heard it first when he blocked my way as I was walking out with my kit bundle under one arm, and while looking round the room as though what was passing his lips had to be treated as secret, he just about got up enough volume for me to understand that he was inviting me to have a look over his 'little place' to see if I wanted to work there. My Opponent was dancing; that's the best way I can describe the shambling exhilarated hops that she was performing around us. I kept quiet through ignorance of what I should do next, but she made it clear that I was going to be in for something. Her fingers were scrabbling, tightening the strings in some complicated new pattern, and pulling so hard ... I returned a 'yes' that was quieter even than his question. I drive a car to get home because the tubes are shut.

When Chrissy first left I kept hearing myself saying 'Don't stop!' Perhaps I mesmerised myself by repeating it too often, because I've accepted the burden of the Test. I'm having to study practically full time. I'm making serious work of it. No more humiliating attempts at risking myself with some adrenalin every now and again, robbing the Midnight Shop or the bicycle. Because of my year-and-a-half-long thirst for a result, for freedom, I've had to give up hanging about thinking that I could find a way to turn back, or that maybe my

Opponent would let me off, or that something would happen to her if I waited long enough. I'm trying to push it through, to leap the whole fence, because I've got no choice. It's judo now, three times a week. It is only a training for the real thing, with no actual courage required, but it's a start in that direction, and perhaps it's only Chrissy who can say 'Stop!' With judo the Test-training is administered through a system of gradings and competitions and differently-coloured belts. When you begin to get good and fast, you move off the colours onto the black belts. After that, maybe I'll have found my way out to the other side of all this. As for now, I can measure my results thrice weekly. The journey seems possible; all you have to do is follow the coloured code and you get there. So I've sold it to myself, and the pattern's become quite set. From home to judo to the Club to home. That's my circle, and I run round it wearing my reshaped jacket and driving my bashed-up car.

Whenever Toots steps onto the stage there is a round of sustained cheering, led by those in the know, and compounded by everyone else, caught up in the sudden change in atmosphere. He won't go up unless there's a full house, well warmed-up. That's his privilege. I've only seen him once so far.

I was leaning against the wall up on the top level. The Boy was leaning next to me. If there were any more orders then we'd probably have died of surprise, but I hadn't let him go, in spite of his asking three times. We stayed up by the doors, looking over the dark silhouettes of people's heads.

Apparently Toots always does the same act. This is how it starts: he stands there facing the audience. That's all there is

152

for a considerable time. He waits, expressionless, while people laugh at him. He is unaffected by their laughter. There's not a hint of the show-off in his pose; he's better than that. He looks as though he's standing there for an unimportant reason. It's a ritual that his family have trained themselves to laugh at.

The Boy asked me, 'How d'you meet Toots?'

'At judo,' I replied.

'All that grappling.'

'How d'you mean?'

'Can't be healthy. I think I might like a go.'

'It's dangerous.'

'Oh, is it?' he mooned, making me suffer for saying my bit seriously.

Finally Toots allows himself to speak from the stage. After this long wait, during which he's been rewarding people who are tittering by looking at them incuriously, he says,

'There's nothing to laugh at.'

He hits exactly the right tone, a puzzled, sincere, low-volume little statement. This is his catch-phrase, part of the ritual laughing-stock that the family recognise and approve of. Next he moves closer to the front of the stage, and scans the audience. His giant robes slope off his chest and fall from his stomach straight to the floor. 'There are some people in to-night,' he says, 'that laugh at nothing. They don't need nothing.' He looks at individuals in the audience, noticing the few who are laughing in an embarrassed way. They sound like strange birds with a nervous call in the silence. 'You don't believe me?' asks Toots. He steps down then off the stage and begins to walk slowly amongst the tables on the first level. Every now and again he stops to look at someone. He takes

153

them straight in the eye with his curious deadpan expression. He is treating them the same as any object: the tables, the chairs. When someone starts laughing he turns and finds it, coursing to the laugh, oblivious to knocking into the backs of people who are drinking. He needs a wide path. It's a girl, helpless with frightened laughter, collapsing onto the lap of her friend.

'Here's one of them,' says Toots to the whole room. A round of clapping grows and then dies away to allow people to hear what Toots is saying to her. 'What are you laughing at?' She can't answer, she's out of control, folded over her friend, hiding her face, shaking. 'It's nothing . . .' says Toots, 'she's laughing at nothing. I ain't told no jokes about in-out . . .' Toots makes an obscene roll with his hips . . . 'I ain't done my tummy dance . . .' When he's finished gyrating in front of her, he returns to the stage.

I've been thinking about the Boy and what he said about the 'serious' amount of money I was earning, so I ask him then:

'How much did the last chef get paid?'

'Not as much as you, that's certain. I wonder why?'

'Because I'll earn it. Get this place going.'

The Boy looks amused and slides his back down the wall to squat. He despises me but I still haven't got to the bottom of it. He's a blotch-faced purblind patty.

Toots is continuing down on the stage. 'Some people,' he lectures, 'need a bit of prompting. Can't be too clever now, with all that drink in your blood. Just a word or two, that's enough. Now I met a man earlier, who ask for something. I don't object to requests. I can do that. He ask me to say this one word. VASECTOMY. Is the man out there tonight who want to laugh at vasectomy?' Toots chooses someone who's laughing and lifts his bulk up the stairs to the third level. People move quickly because of the carelessness of his passage. He evicts a girl who's sitting next to the laughing man and sinks into the chair himself, having drawn it up close. 'Vasectomy,' he intones, as though testing a microphone, 'vasectomy vasectomy.' The man is helpless. Suddenly Toots stands and shouts way above the volume of laughter, 'You must confront it, man!' The audience shouts approval. When he sits again he continues in a more animated, overexcited way, 'What is it about vasectomy? D'you want to have a vasectomy? What if I tell you what's it about, that it's the surgical removal of part of each ... no? You don't want a vasectomy?' Toots takes the man's shoulders in his hands and comforts him, massaging the embarrassed man. 'There, you get used to it ... No one going to come and cut you; you get used to it, vasectomy, vasectomy ... see? You get used to it ...' When Toots stands up to leave, the audience begin wildly shouting out their own words and laughing. 'Knob!' shouts a thin man, leaning over the third-level balcony, 'Knob! ... KNOB!' Toots takes no notice. He has given his signal to the D.J. box. He doesn't finish off his act by taking applause. He sits down and starts to talk to someone he knows, without any seam or break in his behaviour. He remains consistently on one line.

Music drowned out the scene he left behind, and the Boy levered himself out of his squatting position, looking restless and uncomfortable. It was then that I got the big clue. He said to me:

'You be careful, taking all that money.'

'What d'you mean?'

'I should know.'

'What should you know?'

'It's his revenge, see. He eats white meat for breakfast.'

The Boy was flushed from the heat. I resented his oily watching of me. I still wasn't certain about the clue then, what he meant, why he was frightened of me.

'Busy, innit?' he shouted at me, crossing over on his way back to the kitchen. I could feel my chest vibrating off the bass-line of the music. I followed the Boy into the kitchen, wanting to win more clues. I got one, a bit later.

'Nobody's eating,' I said, and he replied:

'Nah, they don't come here to eat.'

Those being the exact words that Toots had used on my first day, I began to see the homosexual shape of their situation.

It's confusing, but there is some kudos for me in being chosen as Toots' Cinderella in the kitchen. At the same time it's revolting, making me angry that I took the job, especially after the warm break of that fart on my chest ... It's my favourite: a demeaning challenge.

Toots must have worked up his courage from a savage will-power ethic. Is it possible that if you pump up your determination violently enough for long enough, you can get to be beyond needing it? The determination would no longer show, it would have been eroded by confidence. Toots has done that, it seems to me. He possesses a solid internal muscle of consistent courage that seems unshakeable. I'm still at the stage of only having the determination, and even with that, I'm a victim of it, I don't really want it. I wish it wasn't there, but the pressure's buckled fast across my chest; the Opponent's made sure of that whether I like it or not. Often I feel it mounting, a great mass of determination; it's my laborious task to capture and harness it.

My routine has changed, working so long into the night. Often I don't wake until the sound of the schoolchildren coming home invades my sleep. My body always feels stiff and tired for the first half-hour, something new that must be a part of working in clubland.

There's one particular shout that often gets me up, possibly more frequently than any other because it's repeated for longer. It comes from way down below on the ground: 'Fidget . . . FIDGET!!' I always draw the curtains and lean out because it amuses me to watch this little show. There he is, a scrubby schoolboy, far below, dashing in short bursts and then stopping to put his hands on his hips. The little dog scurries in front of him, sniffing and charging here and there, always avoiding the clutches of the boy at the last minute. The kid can certainly get some power in his voice. He takes a double-lungful of air and stamps his foot and *bellows* the dog's name: 'FIDGE . . . IT!!' Fidget is only a short distance away and knows his name; that's not the problem. But invariably he wags his tail and stays put, and if the scrubby schoolboy comes closer he'll dash off in a surprise direction. The thing is, Fidget would dearly love to go up and be caught by the little boy, but when he does he gets beaten for not having come sooner. The little dog understands only that when the scrubby schoolboy comes to get him, it's always for a good beating. It's an incomprehensible injustice. The dog sits up against the fence, brushing his tail in the dust and nervously treading the ground with his front feet. The kid is coming. Fidget finally decides to submit to the mystery punishment. He puts on a brave little face, but his agitation increases as the kid gets closer. Sure enough, the boy enforces the usual rule with his curled knuckles before taking the bewildered dog indoors.

157

Looking down on this scene, which happens most afternoons, gives me a more good-humoured idea of what a waste ground the place is. The gap in understanding between the boy and the dog is as desolate as the broken tarmac between the blocks of flats, but the ritual has a comforting absurdity.

From the window I can look down onto the roof of my car. It has not yet been damaged by football, but I wouldn't mind if it was. I've bought a football-proof motor. Every panel already banged in. Even the roof has a dent in it. I admire the bravado of the old geezer downstairs who has to rush out and bawl his head off at the kids when their play drifts near his immaculate Ford Escort.

My car is making a strange popping noise. I should go down and try one more fiddle with it. It sounds like a row of baked potatoes exploding in the boot whenever I lift my foot off the accelerator.

In the dirty washing pile I find two old bits of garment and then without tea I take the bag of tools and leave. The concrete sets of stairs shake me awake on the way down. The old lady in the drawer in my stomach curses and blames the usual people. Oh yes, she's moaning and spitting and shrieking to be let out.

It's a bright August afternoon. Everything is sharply focused. You can see the air moving; even the oxygen is derelict. The cars in the car-park stand in rows like so many tin boxes. The blocks of flats are standing only because of the proudness of their names: Livingstone, Sassoon, Mandela. The old woman struggling along the walkway with the pram looks deserted: a human with no human interest. The pram is full of shopping, a tip of brightly coloured labels – splashes of slogans and free offers. She looks very thin on it.

158

The engine is cool to my touch. I have to take the top of the carburettor off, but for a while it refuses to budge. The surfaces are clamped together. My car is refusing to wake up. It's afraid of the sky because somewhere, under this selfsame patch, the US is meeting the UK to discuss nuclear disarmament and the Nato alliance. Meanwhile I resort to ramming the screwdriver into the joint until it breaks open. Inside lie the delicate float mechanisms and the needle and jets. I'm looking for any dirt that may have got in.

My fingers are becoming duds because of the oil and petrol. As my breath comes short and difficult because of the effort of bending over all the time, I only speak the words of songs that otherwise I might have sung if I'd been a nightclub entertainer:

> Saving my car from the popping noise
> while the President wags his talking chin;
> look the clear blue sky in his eyes;
> don't make no popping noise, President man,
> don't make no noise nowhere . . .

Time is very slippery. There's so much in it that's repeated, yet it's never anything but laid down brand-new. The last time I had a car was over two years ago, when I was still the man I wanted to be. The car had died in this very car-park, but not before long and involved death-throes. My brother Paul saw the last-ditch attempt, on his visit from Oz. He was in the lounge, standing in the middle of the empty room in his overcoat and gloves like an estate agent, when I walked into the flat with half an engine in my arms. I was out of breath from the stairs and in pain from the metal cutting through my sleeves. He stepped forward with an idea that he ought to help, but he remained uselessly suspended in his coat. It suited him, anyway, there was that. He said:

'Shame the lift's broken,' in his slight accent.

'It's never worked,' I replied, proud of it then.

Paul looked gloomy at the thought. Then he said something strange: 'You know, when I think of your lifestyle here it gives me a rising feeling of hysteria.'

I was doubly chuffed when he said that, I remember. How odd! But the memory of him now is suddenly very small, as though the perspective of time has a similar effect to perspective in space. He stood in the middle of the room, hugging his overcoat, hundreds of feet up in the air, without a lift, the estate agent who never knew before that buildings could go up that high. There's nothing to hold onto in my flat. No wonder he was sick with vertigo.

It could be that my car is going to live a bit longer.

October 31

Toots dispenses advice in the early evening, like it's his surgery for the staff's life-problems. Not that he gives any impression of caring. He demands confidences, ragged, clumsy titbits of effort, because he sits there, not contributing, bored-looking, so you're given the feeling of being on the spot, having to feed him with something to keep his gaze from sliding over you. When you come up with something it's always personal and difficult, because if you gave him boring old 'colder today' you'd get less than nothing back. As it is I got the idea for what to do about Chrissy from him, in one gruff sentence. It didn't figure in his expression that I was identifying to him the sex interest in my life, but then nothing ever does figure in his expression; it's cast, and that's it. His advice was unbiased, and almost like a command.

So, that late afternoon Tony is pulling all the bikes in from the outside racks because it's nearly closing time, and I can't help him because I'm busy checking every person that walks past his shop. It has become more difficult in the last half-hour. The volume of people has increased as we move into the allotted going-home time and I have to do both sides of the pavement. Chrissy must not slip through the net; we have unfinished business.

It's staggering that I could have spent all that time planning the perfect theft of one of Tony's outside bikes and yet not noticed that none of them have any pedals fitted. I would have got on the bike and wobbled along for a few yards with my feet plunging uselessly in mid air, and then I would have fallen off and been arrested. Instead Tony strangled me, I went to judo, and now I am working for Toots.

When the day's business is done and the outside door is locked against the public Tony joins me behind the glass that separates us from them. He asks:

'No sign of her?'

'No.'

'Well it was always unlikely, wasn't it?'

'Yes, you're right, Tony. It was unlikely from the very beginning.'

Tony will never be a friend. I wouldn't let him. It's because of this that I resented giving him the details necessary to get his co-operation. I never confessed the entire truth to him. I've locked that up all right, where even I can't get at it before

161

feeling dizzy or falling into a maze. But the odd fact, dressed up as gossip, was to pass my lips that night, and was useful too, keeping him on my side. I don't like him, and I dare say he doesn't like me, but that night we played like friends. I ask him:

'How often d'you see her?'

'She would generally pass by here a bit later, sometime after I've shut up shop.'

'I reckon you're right. She would get home a lot later than this, more often than not. Still, if you do see her sometimes . . .'

'Oh yes, I've seen her since . . . you know.'

'Maybe I could come back, on a Friday maybe, when it's more likely that she's heading off wherever earlier.'

'I don't mind staying on here for a bit, see if you can catch hold of her. I've got some cans in the fridge.'

'You don't have to. You can lend me the keys if you like, and I'll lock up.'

'Can't do that, because of the insurance. I don't mind staying. Tinny?'

'All right then.'

We talk like a couple of mates, perching our cans on the saddles of nearby bikes. I'm busy checking the pedestrians, the words flowing smoothly, but like in someone else's voice, a mate's voice, talking about getting the girl, no, not getting her back, it's not that this voice ever wants a girl *back* . . . just some unfinished business, something to clear up before telling her to push off again. To have been there alone would have been better, I'd be feeling emotional, and true to myself. It would have been good without him there. I'd have seen her; I'd have been rewarded for being in that mood.

Later, after all hope of seeing Chrissy has long gone, we have retired to the office at the back of the shop. It's late, and dark outside now, and my head is humming with the alcohol we have collected on two trips to the off-licence. I'm leaning on the cabinet, where, on that fateful day, I first saw my wallet after recovering consciousness. I'm not sure if Tony is giving me his full attention. We are both queuing up to say things, and listening only to our own voices when they spill into the tiny office. Still, we look at each other and laugh. We are both so funny! So what if interruptions come when they're not quite wanted, never mind! We carry on, our conversation loud and satisfying. We're not completely drowned if a train goes past over the top of us, because it's a challenge to surf through the noise. It gives our sentences an illogical emphasis, when we suddenly have to shout. It's been quite funny, that, a few times. I can tell that Tony's coming up to the finish of his turn: '. . . so all girls come from the sea because they smell like fish from their fannies . . .!'

Now it's my go, and I carry on from where I was before:

'I'd fancied her for ages, see . . .' I say, in my voice that's specially for him on this occasion, 'I'd seen her round the place; a really tight, neat figure, and I'd always thought I'd like to have a go. But, like as usual, you know, when you go up and try and speak to her she doesn't want to say anything back to some . . . some . . .'

'Last thing she wants!' came his interruption, taking over from my blank spot over a word to describe myself. 'Last thing! To speak to some rat-arsed lunatic! I . . . as for me . . . I remember . . .'

While Tony has his turn I sink back to a memory which is

163

made sticky and sentimental by the beer: I remember opening the door to my prospective tenant. There was a sudden surprise, like a wave that picks you up off your feet. It had left me unsteady, standing in the doorway. I learnt her name ... without even having to ask! It came out as part of the normal introductory politeness: Chrissy. She had sprung the trap ... Chrissy.

Tony is doing an impression of his girlfriend's face on the occasion of their first love-making when the train thunders overhead, leaving him girning underneath the noise. Watching his funny face I think, 'I'll never have her again', and it seems like all the good luck that fell into place when she turned up at my door that time has not just been used up, but turned against me. When the noise of the train fades I come in for my turn.

'Well, with me, it just happened – luck. I was looking for a tenant, a mug with money. Why pay the rent when you can get someone else to do it? I had loads of ads out, in the little shops, in the local papers, in the listings mags ...'

'Ads in the national Press, ads in the world Press ...'

'Ads on the telly, yes, and I wore a sandwich-board.'

'A sandwich-board? What's a sandwich like when it's bored, then?'

'It goes all limp and the filling falls out.'

'It's no wonder a sandwich gets bored. All that hanging about.'

'Yes, a lot of waiting about for a sandwich. Hanging out just to get eaten.'

'What was it about Chrissy anyway? You fancied it, did you, a bit of fish?'

'Yup. Imagine, suddenly, I open the door, and there she is,

164

a bloody great fish and pickle sandwich, there on the doorstep.'

'What, pickle as well?'

'I couldn't believe it!'

Then there's our joint effort at a laugh, and he's carrying on with something or other. The memory of Chrissy is like a slight headache behind all this now, because of the injustice I'm doing to it with Tony, of all people.

Chrissy looked exhausted when I saw her more clearly in the light of my hallway. There was no hint of a mark on her face. When she did talk it was an effort. She avoided my eyes, but when I momentarily managed to catch hers I could see there was a question she was asking herself. Her attention flicked over things, and then every so often came back to me, briefly resting, asking that same invisible question . . . She was shopping. I was desperate to fit the bill, to be allowed to look after her. She asked for details, walking round the flat. I followed her, giving answers. She was sharp and sussed. I had an immense respect for her. She'd not been long out of the Screaming Maisonette, and her weariness didn't lack bravery. I wasn't brave enough to look as unhappy as she did. I was overwhelmed by the amount of kindness I suddenly found in myself, that I wanted to give her. The respect that I had for her made me think myself bland. I looked for an opportunity to make an effort. She said:

'If I want to bring a few bits and pieces, would it be all right to put them in here?'

'I'm sorry, no. This room has got to be kept deserted.' That was my attempt, and it resulted in us giving each other a weak smile. She took the room because she had to.

There came an end to that night of waiting to catch Chrissy and getting nothing but the twinge of her memory. As we walk home Tony is informing strangers that we are looking for a sandwich.

'Fish and pickle,' he says, bellicose, eager to defy their realism, 'a sandwich! Called Chrissy . . . if you see her . . .'

The strangers shy off from his approach, but they're accustomed enough to drunks. I trail behind him. I'm grateful for the company, but embarrassed at his antics. When he offers me a lift home in the Stag I spend a brief moment trying to balance a sum out of the different sorts of fear, and then I have to choose to walk.

It was a bad end to the day.

December 10

I'm sitting at a white desk in a white room and there are several bits of paper around me. Some of them are harmless: the newly-designed menu, very professionally done, and the plastic-coated recipe cards that I've been looking through. There's one other bit that's not harmless; it's part of a sheet torn out of a writing pad. I look at it often, since I've got the time. It's a badly-folded scrap of lined paper with the words written on it in pencil. This piece of paper is different. If I am in training for the Test, then it could be called an exam paper, set by someone I've never even met.

My car finally dropped a valve insert, and is all but refusing to carry on. Every journey is an insult to mechanical tolerance; each time I reach a destination it might be the end of the road. I took this as an excuse to tell Toots that I could no longer work for him. I said it was pointless to work in a kitchen with no one ordering anything to eat, and very soon now I'd have to walk home or pay for a taxi; it was impossible; I was bored hanging about doing nothing.

Toots didn't take it; that's the best way I can convey to you what happened. He wasn't receiving. He sat still while I arranged my argument round him. No response. What was happening in that giant ball of a head? I know it went in, because of what happened later.

We are sitting round a table in the bar, a bit later in the week, when there's this conversation. There's me, Toots, and Nick. Nick is only five foot four but he's a fourth *dan* and he used to be South-East champion in the under seventy kilo class. His speciality is a left-handed *seionage* which he can twist into with a fucking invisible speed. (I didn't see him anyway; he just dropped out of sight and I was flying upside down through the arc of a comfortable throw.) That's when somebody's good, when it's fast, hard, and comfortable. Toots had just glided over from the bar and lowered himself into the seat next to me. I am lifted by a wheeze from the cushion. Behind him the barman is cleaning up, still moving with unbroken pace although the punters have gone. He's in haste to get home. The dry mist of cigarette smoke is being diluted with real air from outside the open doors, which hang ready for his fast-walking exit. The waitresses have already scattered into taxis. The Boy is sitting on the other side of the room, looking through a comic without trying.

Toots is sitting next to me. Now all I have to do is deal with the weird pride that comes at these moments and then I'll be able to deal with the hate easily. There are two Items there,

167

slung round the low table. The old lady has had to be strapped into her bed in the drawer. She's right in the middle of me. From time to time she makes renewed efforts to eat through the straps, and then she gives up and resorts to twisting from side to side. She's been a very old lady from birth, she has. Her hair is falling out, yet she has the energy of an insane demon. I wonder if these two males could get any hint, even if they're supernaturally observant, that this is what I'm possessed with when they're this near.

So there's Toots, not saying a word. He takes out an immaculately tooled wallet and shifts the contents out onto the table. We watch as he chops the granules, working the drug into three white ridges with a blade set in a tortoiseshell grip. He takes the first line for himself and then says, handing it to Nick:

'I think we have to do something.'

He sniffs and looks at us, deadpan and unexcited. 'Probably not much,' he adds.

The mirror is passed to me by Nick, who throws in his words like a winning trick at cards: 'Easy. No bother. Almost nothing will be enough.' I push the mirror on to Toots. I don't want drugs off the fat cunt. He's not surprised. He picks up the bank-roll and makes a sharp noise through his nose, like the death of a Hoover.

'D'you want a drink?' he asks me.

'No thanks.' Maybe taking anything is a small slip into weakness or debt.

'I like to look after my people. You eaten?'

'I'm fine. I'm all right.'

(The old rag-lady screeches there, listening to those words 'I'm all right', and breaks her own fingernail, punishing

168

herself for not being taken into account. Then she's left cough-
ing onto the pillow with her mouth dangling, and it's the
dribble from her lip, is it, that's spreading a stain of hun-
ger in my stomach? Perhaps if I eat something, it'll swamp
her.)

'You going to come?' asks Toots, you'd think questioning
the photos of former cabaret stars hanging on the wall, except
for a sly, chance meeting of my eye.

'I don't mind.'

'You don't have to.' He's not being rude or sarcastic. He is
straightforward. After all, he is enough by himself. I've not
got my jacket on. Inside me the old lady is trying to escape,
struggling to volunteer me with both hands raised.

'No, I'll come.'

'More the merrier,' replies Toots, blandly, not merry at all.
Could he ever be? He's packing away his wallet, passing it
somewhere into his clothing, almost like a conjuror with over-
size sleight of hand.

'What's the story?' he asks, at the same time as the barman
passes behind us heading for the doors and home as usual.
With him gone the night settles a notch, and I clunk deeper
into the loneliness of this impending examination, this Test of
the Test that I've been entered for. Can you believe it? I look at
Toots, and from him I try to work up the belief that I'm not
going to have to go through too many of these examinations
before I can qualify up to his level and escape.

We three listen to ourselves. As the story unfolds, they feel
superior to it, I can tell from the tilt of their heads.

'She's worked here for six months,' says Nick, putting
something together for consideration by the conference.

'She's family,' agrees Toots.

'There's a guy. They went out for a year or more. She wanted out, she got bored or whatever. He can't take it.'

Toots stretches both his hands out along the back of the seats, which squeak comically.

'What's the bother?' he asks, without any of the gluttonous fearful curiosity that I've got. He asks it like he might ask 'What's the time?'

'He waits for her to come in from here. Then he comes in to check up on her. Letters, contraceptive gear, anyone else's clothes. Stains and such. It changes, what he looks for, every night.'

'Why hasn't she swapped the locks?'

'She did that, way back. So he broke the window and ran a knife through all her clothes. Cheaper to let him in.'

A knife . . . *Knife* . . . the word goes in so deep, so easily. The old hag of a woman is suddenly stiff and smelly like a dead bird in her drawer. She's staring at the point of the Item. Her energy is chilled by it, frozen, preserved at its highest point. Her blood will stop with excitement at the sight of a dagger, and as long as their blood is fresh, she'll accept anyone's, for the warmth of it.

Toots' hand appears from behind and rests on my shoulder. 'We send this one in,' he says. 'He's fierce enough to send me running, when he comes over all apeshit in the *dojo*.'

Nick smiles at me, curious as to how I'm taking it. I'm determined to withstand the hand on my shoulder. I resent the fact that I need the pride, that I'm sucking it up greedily. I could wear this hand on my shoulder all the time. The hand has a lascivious, valuable weight. The fingers, those fat fingers, they would be like a row of medals, hanging limply.

'When do we go?' asks Nick, the South-East champion.

170

'We send a warning first. Then we move if he takes no notice.'

Later we get up to make tracks. Toots gets his keys from the office, and comes back shouting, 'Boy!' and the Boy, looking steamed up from work, struggles out from where he'd sunk into the chair with waiting so long. 'Get the car,' says Toots, and throws the keys. The Boy makes a show of not catching them, but this display is wasted on Toots. We all know this is the high spot in the Boy's night.

Toots asks me then, 'Your wheels turning?' After I've said maybe and done the first cough of a laugh I go to the cloak-room and find my coat waiting tethered to its peg. I'm going to be glad not to have to force any more confidence tonight. I've been trading in a foreign language; I had no right to sell myself as conversant in their talk, God knows . . . ! Each short phrase that I've said has had a whole soggy mess underneath it, no sub-text of experience, and underneath that, the old lady has been writhing about, despite broken bones. She had done the damage by getting overexcited, and she'd carried on regard-less until petrified at the summit of her delight with the men-tion of the Item slicing through the clothes, and that's how she's stayed. I shrug into my coat and pull the buckle tight over her. My coat is self-sufficient, and I'd better stay in it.

The next bit happens outside, where the whole length of the street is asleep in the damp mild easiness. The weather goes affable on us sometimes, even at this time of year. Everything asleep, even the puddles, but that's except for the Boy. He is enjoying a lounge against Toots' car. The engine is running and the door's open. He looks over at my car with half a sneer, and my car, parked on the pavement, looks too bruised to care. The Boy leans his gaze back to me.

'Does it work?' he asks.

'Better than you do. Quicker. More efficient,' I reply. He comes over and tries again: 'Why's it all so bashed up?'

'Someone's been playing football with it.'

Toots joins us, walking over on shoes that are curling up at the toe because of the weight transferred at the other end through his heel. He surveys the scene: my limp, damaged, apologetic car, me defending it, the Boy tapping one of the indicators with the point of his shoe, delighted that it's hanging by its wires.

'When this thing gives up,' Toots says, gesturing to the ground just below the front bumper; and then surprisingly he stops, his heavy hand as well, suspended at the end of a colourful sleeve. He turns to look at me, full square, his eyes peeping out from on top of the hummocky cheeks, the brow drawing down to frown. Guess what it was. What d'you think, a heart attack? Had he suddenly remembered something? Was he upset? None of these things; I think he must have stopped in surprise – he'd shocked himself, because he'd felt something bubbling up from his giant bag of guts, something . . . could it be, yes . . . incredible, it was a laugh! Toots laughed, not looking anywhere but at me, and it came out high and childish, and so thoroughly *pleased* with itself! It stuttered and wheezed out into the empty night, so rare a thing as to make the Boy stop his kicking of my indicator and take up gawping at him instead. What a turn around this was! That laugh, it was like a libation, a drink-offering, but in reverse, not given in supplication to a god, but instead received, from Toots, one laugh, received with amazed pleasure.

So that's how it comes to be that I'm sitting writing this at a different table in another part of town, because Toots, while turning back to his car (still laughing), called over his shoulder that there was a room at his house, if my wheels gave out and I needed help. 'Cheap rent,' he said, barking the words conversationally, 'free lift to work.' Then he was raising his arms in the air and swaying from side to side as though there was music somewhere.

As it turned out it wasn't my car that gave out, it was me. The car will be parked in the square of tarmac below my flat, still waiting, I dare hope, for my return. As for me, I gave myself up to some illness; a message surfaced in my mind, when I was at the epicentre of my sickness, that illness had been queuing up, ready to come in, like the thread of dressed-up club-goers on Saturdays, and because I'd momentarily forgotten to keep increasing the pressure of my shoulder against the door, illness had squeezed in.

It was after the call from the removal men that I fell sick. Their heavy, practised banging on the door came before I was awake, in the early afternoon. The Window Check: two shadows, male. The spyhole gave me two bloated males in ballooning overalls. They convinced me enough to open the door because they were smoking and laughing together. The larger of the two read my name out from a formal square of paper, and looked at me to see if I was responsible for this name.

'Yes,' I replied.

'We've come for the comfies.'

'What?'

He looked at his paper again. 'Miss . . . Miss Chrissy Boxer. She should have squared it with you for us to come and pick up her comfies.'

'Oh. Yes, she did. Come in. This way.'

'There's a settee and two chairs, mate, according to my orders from Adolf back at the office.'

'That's right. There they are.'

So Chrissy did exist somewhere, doing her bit under this same round of day and night, except doing it the right way up, like these two. I was off my guard, half asleep. The illness must have been getting a foot in the door right then.

It was insulting, some of the comments that guy made, the way he called me 'mate' while at the same time looking at me like I was the last crumbling lump of hard cheese in a relationship that had gone bankrupt; and here he was, Mr Important Removal Man, with a part to play, on the side of the girl. I could see his thoughts running: 'So this guy's lost his girl, that means there's a girl on the loose . . . should meet her the other end . . .' Maybe he'd make a move, if the girl turned out all right when he delivered. He could be a cousin to Mr Popupandseeme; maybe Mr Bargeinandfuckit or Mr Fuck'emfeedyourfaceandforget'em.

'Don't worry, mate,' he said as he was walking backwards with his neck stringing to lift the weight, 'there's plenty more puddles to piddle in!'

I was standing dumbly, caught out by this business, half wanting to help, wholly wanting to have the courage to rage with anger and refuse access to the bloody comfies. Another bit of my life was going backwards, carried out by him and his straining forearms.

I had a cue and was ready to take it; it would come when they were carrying the last chair out. I was lying in wait in the wing of the doorway, with my own made-up words.

174

'That's it then, mate,' he said, as expected. 'Don't hang about – get yourself a job, and then you'll get another girl, then get yourself another suite, and give us a call to move it for you.'

'Have you got her address?' I asked; the beginning of the trick.

'Yup. All set. Bye then.' The two of them set their feet shifting again, like puppets glued to the chair.

'It's a new address. I ought to check you've got it right.'

'Oh, we've got the address.'

'What, Clapham Road?' I was talking cheerfully, directly, forcing the plan through. The two of them stopped again. The smaller man turned to look at me as well. He wore a weary face.

'I'm sorry, sir,' said the larger one from his end, 'but I'm under instruction not to tell you the address. Apparently the other party didn't want you to know her address. Don't blame me, it's Adolf back at the office, but I have to follow along with the orders . . .'

I had to rush to stop the man from being embarrassed and superior to me. 'No, of course,' I said, earnestly and honourably, as they disappeared over the tip of the stairs, 'quite right, that . . .' There was nothing I could add to let myself off the hook. The only mercy came when I had closed the door behind them. They were probably already starting to make up the joke lines and insults about me. The thought of that, as I stood in the emptier lounge, made a blanket of coldness touch my skin through the dressing-gown, and I shivered to throw it off, and then sneezed, sending a thousand million wet motes of snot and saliva into the air at breakneck speed. A sneeze makes the chill really sit on you when you're about to be ill;

175

the sickness can then throw a cramping grip on the back of your neck and shake you by the scruff.

Back in bed and lying still to prevent the duvet moving any air over my skin, I gave some time to thinking about Chrissy deliberately covering her tracks like that to keep me away from her. I had written a reply to her note, a long one, maybe too long, so the ball was in her court, if it was in court at all. But there had been nothing from her, even though she was the one who wanted me to answer her. What had my letter done to her? Was she revolted by it? Angry? What was going on out there, that was everything to do with me, but which I wasn't allowed anywhere near? Would it hurt me? Again I tried to remember the details of my reply, examining the thread of it for any potential misunderstanding which might have caused her to block me out.

Later on, when the planet had spun us into an evening as wet as any other, I decamped from the bed and carried my duvet on my back like a stripy cotton beetle to the lounge, where I perched on the hard chair next to the phone. I was trying to decide what to tell Toots. I had been dragged to a low ebb by those removal men. They had unsettled me. I was a stranger amongst strangers; and yet they still *knew* . . .

Everyone looks ugly, don't they, sometimes? I am still ugly, in tune with ugliness, because I've been sick. Life has been cheap and damaging during these last five days at Toots' house; but I remember, from being ill before, that it can be wonderful when you're better, for a while anyway. Wonderful happens when Horrible is taken away. Wonderful is kind of spring-loaded, or automatic. It seems to me like another one of life's tricks.

So I picked up the phone and told Toots I was going to be ill, and then I looked for a while at the new moving picture, the Figure Washing Up. There she was, in and out of her red frame as usual, spectacularly overlit by a light bulb above her head, carrying in the ramshackle piles of dishes. A lonely job, washing up for all those family mouths.

I don't know how much you do to make yourself lonely. The more the sort of people around me, like the removal men and the parking meter office and the taxman and the washing-up woman, the more they conspire to interfere, the more conniving I become at sampling my own isolation. I can't tell you how heavily I had weighted myself when I returned to bed after the phone call; I was very, very, stupidly Chrissyless, I was as low as a groan. I crept back to bed, wearing as near as anything that expression on the trout's face when you press the edge of the Item into its gill: it opens its mouth in a dead gape, and looks as though it suspected it could be this bad all along. No surprise, not even the thrill of a horrible surprise, just plain, dull, sick-bed loneliness, pressing into the side of my neck.

It was Nick who turned up to take me over to Toots' place. He came like another removal man, with a more fragile load to deal with. I went; and I'm still here, sitting at a modern white desk which looks as though it's never been used. Nearly everything in Toots' house is like that. As soon as it's used, it's returned to pristine showroom condition. Even the flannels are hung on the radiators to make them dry and square when you come to use them again.

The first night I arrived I was steered into the bedroom by Nick. Dutiful sick-porter that he was, he didn't try anything polite and just retired soundlessly back over the white carpet. I heard nothing except for the chinking car keys and the dull vibration sent up by his closing the front door. I was alone in the house. Alone, lonely, unattended, separated, unattached, no hand to press my brow. The bed was bolstered high with cushions, topped and tailed with brass railings. I got in and strayed into pre-sleep.

It's at times like these that I am most at risk from the fever of difficult challenges. How your thoughts can boil with self-adjusting facts, just before you drop into the complete opposite, the mystery of sleep.

Of course I am thinking about the possibility of this approaching exam with Toots and the waitress's clothes-murdering boyfriend. That situation is at the other end of some leap I'll be prodded into making. Meanwhile I compare it with the Original Incident, as always, so boringly always! For how long will all my daily events follow along this track because I have to boomerang back to that?

Those moments before I had to make my run for the Alley, the events of the Original Incident, are scalded on my memory, and not a day goes past when I don't pick them over, in my automatic kind of way. What kind of ghoul am I, not to be able to switch into automatic forget-mode on this? The logging of the memory will always remain disconnected; fragments of action within what must have been an entire sequence. I have the Item idly waiting, standing in his camelhair overcoat like he's waiting for a bus, with his hands tight in his coat pockets. I have him swaying into my path unexpectedly to ask a polite question about the time, please. I have my over-friendly answer, my last moment of dumb confidence. I don't have his face, or his hands, although I must have seen them clearly when he held my wrist to see the watch for

178

himself. I have the Item's voice, his careless courage, his slouch, and the loud double click of the Item as it flew open on its way out from his pocket. I can see in lurid detail, like I've tinted the memory for special effect, the blade against the underside of my wrist. That is a shivered splinter of a memory, something that I wanted so much not to have happened that I end up re-running it, making it happen over and over as a warning.

When the Item got what he wanted he pushed me off, muttering an insult. When he had gone I angrily strode about, not knowing what to do, like a chicken that's had its head cut off. Just as I was feeling glad that I'd escaped with my jewellery intact, escaped quite lightly, maybe (except, that is, for what was then just a hint, a new something, knowledge, the awful first settling of fear in the eaves), I noticed the wetness and looked down to see that the push had been a deliberate wound, and in the next glance I saw the Item running at me again, accompanied by more males running with him. That's when I turned to chase hard for that short cut home, that bloody gritty cold-infested Alley.

So there was some unhappiness and physical discomfort the first night I was here at Toots'. The past raced back and forth behind my headache, getting overhauled again and again and then being dragged up to the present to be used as a tool for my unstinting guesswork over the future. The past is a doddle to make up theories about. You have had plenty of time to look for a pattern and marshal the appropriate understanding. I still think of those rabbits in Cornwall. I crave their facility for constantly forgetting and thereby being able to rest, and do nothing. They can just get on with eating companionably.

I didn't hear anyone come in that night, and I slept through to the afternoon, adrift on the sweep of my usual clock. I was woken by the Boy, who was standing in the doorway with a plastic washing-up bowl in his hand.

'D'you need this?' he asked.

'No thanks, it will make me feel sick.' My voice was still burred, what with sleeping through so much snot and ache.

'Cup of tea then?'

'Thanks,' I said, and he turned and left. Everyone moves so silently in this place; the carpets are deep enough to soak up any noise. . was enjoying a slight surprise at the sight of the Boy. He was wearing something ridiculous; no wonder he looked like an apology. A sort of jellaba or something, a long striped nightie with a hood. Ha, he was going to suffer while I was here, if that's what he had to go round in.

I didn't know the geography of the place then, but I found out later that I was on the top floor of a four-bedroomed mansion house in a smart Georgian street that had been resurrected out of the pile of leaking Georgian squats and modern council estates surrounding it. The whole of that first day I stayed in bed, briefly visited by Toots and the moron he found at the airport.

I had been having a wander through the dream that I had woken up with still more or less in my possession. Chrissy was wearing a new swimsuit with a fishing-fly stuck in her leg, which gave her pain, but which she could take out—'See, it comes out'—but she wasn't sure if the pus was caused by something else. Anyway, she'd put the fishing-fly back in. That was what I was puzzling over when Toots came in with a young stiff-legged Spanish-looking man behind him.

'This is José,' he said, and turned to José.

180

'It's no important,' said José, speaking the language with difficulty and absolute authority.

'I found him,' continued Toots, 'on his way from the airport, lost in the middle of the night.'

Toots stood looking out through the muslin curtains while José stood behind him, on one leg with his hands crossed in front of his genitals, looking at the curve of Toots' back. He was puzzled, but not as horrified as he would be later. Toots moved over to the bed, the freeholder of this house and also lifetime owner of a fat man's grace in everyday movement. No, you couldn't see his confidence, it was long out of sight. He pressed a hand to my forehead, and considered things around me: the pillows, walls, bedstead, black onyx lampstand.

'Check you out later,' he said softly, and left the room followed by the swaggering José.

I had turned round to the other side of the bed to deal with their visit, and afterwards, before I had had time to heat up the new patch of sheet and pillow, I saw that my clothes had been taken away and now only a housefrock, similar to the Boy's but in a different stripe, was lying across the back of the chair.

The rest of the day passed on its own without me. I did get up once and had to anchor myself to a wall because of the sudden dizziness. I took a few steps and saw various things from the window that Toots and José had been queuing up at earlier. There were workmen in boots floating with difficulty over the mud of a building site opposite. Children on big bright bikes worked out courses for themselves round the cars and on the unguarded edge of the site. There was peace here, an escape available for the children's cries: the silent blue sky. It would be cold out there. No books in the room, no sign of

181

anyone else having been here. No sign that I was here, come to that, with my stuff being taken away like that. Back to the duvet, you can imagine, was more of a fall than a walk.

I got to know my bed very well. The only thing I could have asked for was my girlfriend to weigh me down or read to me.

José appeared in the evening, when I presumed the others had already gone to work. He had with him a bowl of hot soup on a tray. I had been working out why Chrissy dipped the fish-hook in and out of the little wet crater of pus in my dream; was I the crater or the fishing-fly, or both, or was I Chrissy? Not geared for being sociable, anyway.

'You?' he asked, nodding at the soup.

'No thanks.'

He put it down on the table next to the bed.

'I . . . um . . . I bee . . . fore . . .'

'What before?' I asked, sounding condescending like a language teacher.

'No really. I . . .' he started again on this elusive trial of his English. 'Um . . . me . . . myself . . . um . . .' Then he sat on the bed to rack his brains.

'Now, you . . . er . . . mm . . . not . . .' he went, followed by another lapse into wordlessness. After a short while he whispered conversationally, 'It's no important.'

Again we waited. I thought it was a desperate time, but he wanted to carry on trying. 'You, you,' he said, stabbing a finger at me, anxious to get something right. I agreed with him:

'Yes?'

This went on for a much longer bout. When I tried to tell him that I was ill and could he go, for fuck's sake could he go, he didn't understand and thought it was part of the lesson he'd come to learn about England – taking it all in, looking at me with a quizzical, interested expression, and sometimes having the gall to pretend to understand, nodding repeatedly as I told him I was in a bad state and wanted him to leave me alone. Eventually I found myself having a sick weep in front of him. He was shocked. It was no joke. All right, if that's what he wanted, he'd bloody well get it, a real mouthful, then he would go.

'Alone, evacuated, deserted . . .' I shouted, pointing at him, and managing momentarily to push out a more sociable laugh. I talked hard, to stop my breathing from gusting into embarrassing hurricane sobs. 'Me too,' I said, managing it. 'I had a girl, right, a girl; she was on top of everything, on top of anything you could throw at her, on top of me, she was . . . above me, in a funny sort of way, and I had to do something, *had to*, but I don't know why. What for? I think it's all to do with power, isn't it?'

He was listening hard, but didn't hear. I was suddenly romanticising the absurdity of his situation. The swish of the cars outside, this unintelligible sound coming from a sick man in a room in London; this would make an Experience. I would be a long way out from the guidebooks, somewhere else, where we all live.

'It all boils down to power, doesn't it?' I continued, gaining more in self-control now. 'Who makes the tea, who pays for what, who has a friend to go and see or an Experience . . . an Experience . . .'

'Eks . . .' he began, 'Ekspeerents . . .'

'Yes. They are like a . . . a unit of energy, something that adds up, something very valuable in the power stakes. She had had Experience, probably many units of it, and she'd kept
183

her power building up, in spite of how damaging it might have been; maybe she'd got even more power because of how explosive her Experiences were; but me, when I had one Experience, I had my power taken off me, all of it, I was robbed.'

José's bewildered brown eyes were doing a good impression of a concerned, intelligent look. He stopped nodding and looked down at his hands, and next he started a slow shaking of his head instead, just to cover himself. He added a pursing of the lips and a silent whistle of admiration. That would be enough, he obviously thought then, because he got up off the bed and made ready to go.

'It's not important,' I said.

A great smacking smile of relief opened up his face, and he repeated the phrase several times. We both started laughing, and he was delighted. 'It is important,' I said, still laughing at him. 'It is important.'

'Eh?' he asked, his chins folding as he looked down at me.

'It . . .' I said, indicating that he should repeat after me.

'It,' he said, smiling joyfully and oscillating one of his straight legs.

'Is,' I said.

'Iz,' he followed.

'Important!' I said, with a final flourish.

'Importan!' he copied my tone, and laughed. He lifted his hand and left the room repeating, 'It *iz* importan' under his breath. The carpets led him quietly away to some other part of the house.

The next day was still high-pressure brightness and a painful quantity of light was outside my window. The mud on the building site had dried into a scored, corrugated surface which jarred the arms of the circling boy-cyclists. My limbs ached in the middle of the bones and chills fluttered over my skin . . . dreadful. Back to bed. I missed my pictures, and the little boy failing with his dog every afternoon, but it was a good thing to be here, ensconced in privilege. I would have been ploughing through acres of self-pity at home.

The Boy came in at some unknown hour of the day and relayed a message from Toots. José had made a face and pointed upstairs, conveying that he thought I was very ill. Toots had sent the Boy to ask what had happened. The Boy was putting on a very blank face with me, like a servant in a hotel. He had packed away his sneer for good, maybe because I was ill, maybe because I was seeing him in his ridiculous housefrock, or perhaps he thought there was a real danger that he might have to put up with me for a long time. By behaving well towards me, he was begging me not to mention his dress or stay too long. That's how I saw it. Difficult.

I said I was all right, not to worry. I asked for some drink and any books or magazines that were about. The Boy came and went, uncomplaining. For the most part I remained motionless, wondering why I didn't need to go to the bathroom, or eat. The books failed to tease me into their sort of doing nothing. Where was Toots? That must be a big effort, when that man was ill. And if he died, they'd have to rig up scaffolding and build his coffin round him, like a house. Would the vicar be able to muster enough grave-diggers? Or would Toots burn? Perhaps he would gently deflate overnight. Every now and again I thought of getting up, but quashed it because of the prospect of putting on the gown that was folded over the chair. That third day passed, punctuated by the Boy and at the proper time drawn over by the sooty dusk.

On the fourth day, yesterday, I did get up. I asked the Boy for my clothes, and he went and got them, with a slight increase in the baldness of his expression. When I went downstairs, with my knees giving a little too much on each stair, my first surprise was to see José in one of the wretched housefrocks. I laughed at him, and he did a metallic cackle in reply, thinking we were taking up from where we'd left off. He shook my hand, saying, 'Yay . . . yay!' like we were buddies.

Later on in the afternoon I was sitting with Toots and José in the white living-room. I think it's a deliberate ploy by Toots to have this house white, so that he can be the only large palette of colour moving through it. The stripes on the Boy's housefrock were of a suitably thin, beige variety. I was sitting stiffly in an armchair, my neck wobbling precariously, my head threatening to drop off into my lap if I did anything but keep its weight directly above the spine. Toots was sitting on an extraordinary long sofa, next to José, who was watching the television intently, leaning away from Toots.

'This man,' said Toots, curling a thumb towards José, 'came yesterday and made a fuss. He was pointing upstairs, at you, and making faces.'

José had felt the thumb moving next to him on the sofa and had turned to look at it, quick enough to catch the stream of incomprehensible sound coming out of Toots' mouth. The television was rumbling at this point, and someone had just said, 'It's an earthquake.' José looked at the accusing thumb, puzzled.

'I was trying to tell him to go away,' I said, 'and he didn't understand.'

'So?' asked Toots, mildly curious and impatient.

'I got a bit angry.'

'It's funny, innit, how you can say anything to him.'

'It wasn't funny then.'

Toots looked at me, unblinking, his chest rising and falling with the usual amplitude. José had seen that Toots was talking to me, and had turned back to follow the progress of the earthquake. Water was swirling round a gasping virgin as she tried to mount a log.

'José,' said Toots. José looked round sharply. He was ill at ease, uncomfortably on the inside of a housefrock.

'José, I'm going to fuck you later.'

'Mmm?' asked José, as though there was a chance he might understand if Toots spoke louder.

'I'm going to take you upstairs and squash you onto that bed,' said Toots, very loudly.

'Ah . . .' said José.

'I'll show you what you have to do. Later. Some things with your legs. Your hands. OK?'

'OK,' agreed José, patting his chest. 'I OK.' He smiled and went back to the bouncing rocks and terrified villagers on the television. Toots voiced a sigh of content and sank his head onto the back of the chair.

'What's happening with José? Why is he here? Where's he going to go?' I asked.

'Ah . . .' said Toots, and threw up a lazy hand to dismiss the matter. 'And you, what's happening with you? Did you find that girl?'

'Not yet.'

'Did you go find her at work?'

'No. I couldn't do that. I couldn't. I remembered that there was this guy who was trying to get to her at work before. We took turns in despising him. I wasn't going to put myself in the same cage as him. I did take your advice, though; I tried waiting for her, but somewhere else.'

'Where d'you try?' he asked, with a slow-wheeling laugh afterwards, at the thought of someone making such a lot of effort.

'Oh, the tube station. A shop.'

'You wanna sort yourself out, look ahead, where you're going, not backwards. Forget her.'

Then he moved with surprising speed, clapping his hand onto José's leg more like to stop it from moving than as a sign of affection. '*Eh? José?*' he said, and José's spinning face already knew that here it came, the time that he always knew would come, when he would be frightened by this strange man. 'José's never been fucked,' said Toots to José, and moved his hand up José's thigh, kneading it violently. The housecoat was dragged up underneath Toots' hand, the hem rising to show a comical set of black Italian loafers each topped with a crinkled collar of blue sock, and then, as Toots' manipulating hand went higher, the thin hairy goat-legs, still calmly together in a pair, not taking any action yet over this outrageous affront to international diplomacy.

'José, José, it's not important,' said Toots, cruelly. His hand snapped over José's crotch. José panicked instantly, as though on a switch, jumping off the sofa and fighting off the tangle of Toots' arm, issuing a loud cry as a deterrent. He skipped immediately to the furthest corner of the room, glaring at Toots and saying something in Spanish. He couldn't get to the door without passing by Toots on the sofa, so he stood there, cornered, swinging from foot to foot, wearing an angry, un-

188

comprehending expression, like a hunted animal that's been dressed up in human clothes as a joke. Toots turned to me conversationally: 'You ought to try a boy, you know. Very good.'

'They look good when they're scared, don't they?' I said, but it came out sarcastically, because José was so visibly scared and I felt an immediate sympathy.

Seeing that Toots, his captor, was lounging with a careless weighty poise on the sofa, José took the risk of making past him for the door. He disappeared, with a series of clicks from his throat and the flap of the gown round his striding feet.

'No humour,' said Toots, 'boring.'

We stayed together in the room for several hours, watching the television romance developing between the star and the gasping virgin, who had miraculously found a comprehensive wardrobe amongst the rubble. They were patching together a few torn-up earthquake survivors. If I thought of something with humour in it, which happened spasmodically, we'd talk. Often it was mocking the TV film – say, the boiled-eggs bottom of the starlet, or the long bouts of twitching cruelty that the hero's mouth indulged in. After several yawns opening up Toots' head on the sofa I told him about that episode, the one that happened way back, when the boy Gordon was sobbing on the shelf in the Cornwall place, and the subsequent attempt at the business with his nanny in the woods. I drew breath to tell him about my using it against Chrissy, but it didn't come, just a humming growl instead. I didn't want his advice.

I've confided too much in Toots already. When you tell Toots something it's like you've given it away forever. He doesn't leave you with the impression that it's worth much, either. I think that's why you want to keep on giving him more, you want to tip the scales. Some chance, with him sitting on the other end, the fat pig.

I felt much better today, before Toots brought the exam paper. I'd taken part in the small, constant pleasure of filling up with a bit of food, and I was sitting up here at the white table looking at the new menus. There's colour printing, weekly rotation of variety, the works.

Then Toots came in with the bit of paper still in the envelope. We did another bout of off and on conversation, in the usual style. He walked over to me, and I was surprised when he put the envelope into my hand. On it was written 'TO MARIA'S FRIENDS' in large capital letters, with the word 'friends' being twice the size of the others. Mockery. Inside was a note:

> There was a dog called Maria
> And some turds who said they knew her;
> They ganged up on me
> As tough as could be

Across the bottom of the note was printed the final line, again in much bigger writing:

FUCK OFF OUT OF IT YOU BOGHEADS.

Eight

Boiler is spending too long out of the kitchen. He revolts against my company, probably because of my intimacy with Toots. Every day now his trips to 'talk to someone' have become more frequent and long-winded. The kitchen works at such a furious pace, I can't be doing with this behaviour. It's Friday night for God's sake. Chopping vegetables is not my job. I will speak with Toots.

'Toots.'

I'm talking just behind his shoulder while he checks a new video screen show. He turns to look at me with the usual deadpan gaze. He says:

'This is Toots speaking.'

He's already under the spell of his exotic wallet. It's an early start on Friday nights.

'I need the Boy in the kitchen full time now. We're too busy for him to behave like he's used to. Either that or I have to have somebody else.'

'The Boy doesn't like being called Boiler.'

'I'll stop calling him Boiler if he comes back and does the work.'

'No, no. I will tell him from now on his name is Boiler. I'll send him to you.'

Toots' mind is staying somewhere in a different place. His

answer to my problem has provided a moment of amusement for him.

When the Boy comes back to the kitchen he's sulking. He goes straight to the work surface and starts chopping sweet potatoes. I watch him from the corner of my eye wielding one of my Items. He judges the thickness of each slice carefully before making each cut. He is laboriously slow. I begin to remonstrate:

'Boy . . .'

He doesn't reply. I continue:

'You'll cut yourself doing it like that. I've shown you before. Hold your thumb at the back. Put your fingers in a line on top. As you run your fingers backwards to give you the size of the slice, bring the knife down using your fingernails as a guide.'

'I cut myself doing it your way.'

'Then you weren't doing it properly.'

'My name is Boiler. Don't call me Boy.'

I take a sweet potato and show him slowly the way to do it. Then I take a courgette, top and tail it, and chop it fast, slinging the knife down on the board for him.

'There. The bloody thing's dead in two seconds flat. There's that lot to do. Then onions and egg-plant and banana and peppers. All in the bowls. Do it. Fast. Just because you wear a dress at home . . .'

His face is burning in blotches. When I turn my back I hear the smack of the blade against the board. He's pressing too hard, which slows you up.

The kitchen is impossibly small for the increase in work load. There's not enough space for the produce, or for me and Boiler to work quickly and efficiently.

It's a race every Friday night. The patchy-faced swearing

192

Boiler versus the chef without his shirt on. The music bursts through the doors, when they swing open from the stage, to encourage us. It's an unfair race, because I can make up whatever rules I like. I can keep one step ahead by throwing another job at him. There's the vegetables, and laying out the plates and numbering them with the tags made out by the waitresses. If he looks about to finish anything I can shout, 'Wash up!' and have him furiously banging open the machine door. The clash of crockery is ear-splitting.

Now that I see him rest his thin boy's rump against the steel surface, I shout over the top of the hissing food:

'Brandy! And a lager in a jug.'

He has to go for them. I check each dish before the waitress takes it out. They stand tense for two seconds while I scan the plate. By the time they hit the door with their bums they're practically running. If it doesn't look neat I will throw the whole thing in the bin. Boiler will have to set it out again, and retrieve the plate and the tag from amongst the stinking refuse as punishment.

Boiler drinks bitter. It goes straight to his head. His patches of high colour start sweating, and he talks coarsely over the top of the words of songs.

I shout: 'Sweep!' and curse him when he jogs my frying arm as he reaches for the broom. After he's done it I point here and there, to bits that he's missed. I'll keep Boiler on the boil.

He has no stamina. For five hours we work without a break, and towards two o'clock he's drunk, and furious at the mistakes he's making. His neck sticks forward, and from the side you can see how his bottom eyelid comes up higher than usual onto the eyeball. It's that, I think, that gives him the look of a

193

half-bald chicken. Chickens blink from the bottom upwards, only marginally uglier than Boiler.

Boiler has to do all the clearing up. While I sit in the Bar counting the money and drinking with Toots I hear him clanking in the kitchen. The waitresses are taking their shoes off.

When he finally appears he goes for his drink that the barman leaves out for him. He takes it to sit by himself with a comic. He is waiting for the best part of the job: going to get Toots' car and maybe even driving home. Toots and I are talking about him.

When I approach he looks at me with the normal hint of malice and moves off to another seat. I follow.

'Boy . . .'

'My name is Boiler.'

'Boiler.'

'What?'

'I'm going to have another drink. Want one?'

'All right. I haven't finished this one yet, but why not have two? I can drink them both at once. No problem.'

'Another can?'

'No. A whisky.'

'Toots will love you if you smash the car. D'you want water?'

'Of course not.'

By the time I return with the spirits he's finished his tinny. I say:

'We're going to need another chef soon, if this keeps up.'

'Oh yeah?'

'Are you interested in training?'

'No.'

'Why not?'

'I'm not interested in being trained by a racist pig.'

'That was a private conversation, Boiler.'

'I was there.'

'You're always there.'

'So?'

'So you're not interested?'

'I might be.'

'Think about it.'

Boiler is a skin-thin mouldy little twerp.

There has been an unfortunate incident with Tony. I have to sign off from him now. We are not even good companions. We've given it a try and it always just misses. This is how we did the final escape from our so-called friendship, one of those with prescribed greetings, always the same, and a false voice each to remain friendly.

We are waiting for a grading competition. Our suits are clean and stiff against our skins, and the changing-rooms are crowded with strangers coming to try and win a higher belt. The palms of my hands are sweating. I have a nervous cramp in my fingers and a shit ready all the time. From time to time I wipe the palms of my hands slowly and firmly down my trouser legs. Tony asks:

'You do any special training?'

'No. Just the usual. You?'

'None at all. I've not even done the usual.'

I think, 'Liar.' He says, 'Mind you, your usual's a bit more than most, I give you that.'

We join the crowd of people sitting by the side of the mat. The judges will soon select two names of equivalent rank, who then have to step up onto the mat for a three-minute bout.

Whoever wins can look forward to getting his book marked up another grade. I have been prodded unmercifully by the Opponent, railroaded up to second *kyu* – a lower brown belt. But chasing these signatures is only a sport. She has her one-track mind set on something outside.

'You're pretty thick with Toots now, then.'

'I only work for him.'

'How's it going?'

'I'm trying to set up the kitchen so people want to eat the stuff.'

'He's a big rich spade, no mistake. Have you seen his car?'

'No?'

'Porsche. Nine two eight!'

'Yes. I know. I work for him, don't I?'

'Ah. But have you been paid yet?'

'Every week.'

'Good money?'

'Best I ever earnt.'

'I don't like him. He's a rich lump of black, no mistake.'

'You're a racist pig, Tony.'

I drag my hands hard down the length of my thighs. They're left dry. It pleases me to have them hot and tingling. I work at them, stretching and pressing the knuckles. Soon they'll have to win the grip for me.

'I'm definitely not that. Some of my best friends are blacks. I just don't like anyone who's as arrogant as him. Mind you, if one of them came home with my sister I might be a bit offended.'

I'm angry. I'm mad at the winking git. I hate the way his chest has a bony dip in the middle of it.

Tony is proud of the fact that he introduced me to judo. When I got the brown belt he behaved as though he'd trained me all by himself. He's proud of the few times he's seen Chrissy, bringing me the information on her like he's in my employment as a private dick.

On the opposite side of the hall the judges look serious and critical. The one in the middle rises from his official desk and reads two names from a sheet of paper. Two figures from amongst our pack stand up and pick their way to the edge of the mat. They remove their sandals and bow before stepping onto the mat to face each other for the contest. They stand loosely, well trained, at the proper distance. To work at maximum speed and power it's important to be relaxed. The referee checks their clothing and their hands. When he says, '*Re*' they bow and take one step forward, trying to build their internal resolve. At the command '*Hajjime*' they start to circle each other, looking to get the first grip. The smaller player is suggesting some trick; he takes his own suit collar and is offering it to his opponent to hold. The opponent makes a half-move towards it, and finds out that his own arm is in danger of being taken into a trap. He goes in very fast with his other arm and secures the grip. The smaller man is now in trouble.

I put in a low whisper to Tony above the harsh, abrupt breathings of the contestants as they struggle for a throw:

'Did she say who it was that died?'

'What?'

'Who was it that left her the house?'

'I don't know.'

'What sort of house is it?'

'I don't know. It's small. You lost out there, eh?'

'Whereabouts is it?'

'Dunno.'

'Is she seeing her old friends again?'

'No.'

'Only you, every so often.'

'Once in a while she passes by. You ought to try again.'

Tony is following the match. The man who gave his collar away has been suffering ever since, having failed to pull off the arm-lock at the beginning. He steps in deep for *tomoenage*, the ideal small man's throw, sacrificing his own back to the mat. He fails to control the top half of the other man's body, allowing it to twist round and come down on top. He looks like he's had it. His legs thrash, trying to twist out of the hold-down. I can't see his face. I imagine he's suffocating somewhere under there, because he's doing nothing very constructive to get out. Occasionally he bucks this way and that to try and jump out of it. For thirty seconds his back is pinned to the floor. He's lost. I ask Tony:

'What sort of people were they?'

'Who?'

'Her old friends.'

'Ordinary. I mean, what d'you want to know? They could be anyone in this room.'

I look around me. There are plenty of people on the mat this afternoon. The room smells of aftershave and freshly laundered suits. Later it would warm up more with the sweat. I think, 'Half of us are Items.'

Tony and I are chosen together. I get a glimpse of his face settling sternly when he hears his name immediately after mine. We are both going for first *kyu*, but I am several pounds lighter than he is. We've trained together, so we know what to watch out for. He is strong and quick on locking the elbow and strangling; I'm better on the throws. There's no hint that we know each other when we take the bow. We've become impersonal. The referee controls us with precise words. We're both making the effort to relax at the height of our concentration. We've been trained to make sense out of the anarchy of fighting, without ever being allowed to go as far as the real anarchy. He tells us, with a smart whip of a word, to start. From the beginning, we try for our favourite deceptions.

When I get Tony down in a scarf hold without winning any points on the throw, I know I'm in a dangerous position; he is stronger on the ground than I am. I jam my shoulder hard under his chin, and curl the hand that's underneath his neck into a fist. I'm squeezing the adenoidal artery situated in the rear corner of his neck onto the cutting edge of my fist, with the mat catching the entire load of pressure from my action.

He should have submitted. When I stand up the referee stops me from checking on him and takes me over to the edge of the mat and tells me to wait there. They have turned him over on his side; I can see the limp curves of his legs in the baggy white trousers. The doctor is checking his pulse in the abnormally quiet room. I'm worried. I feel guilty, standing here, sent to the corner like a schoolboy. I'm also aware that I might be dangerous. I must be dangerous. Look at him. I've got him down and unconscious in a minute and a half.

Tony is recovering. They help him into the changing room. I take my bow alone in front of the referee, and step backwards off the mat in the proper way. I have won all I need to. I am first *kyu*, ready to start trying for black.

In the changing room Tony accuses me of trying to pursue a vendetta against him on account of the bicycle-stealing in-

199

cident. I point out that he failed to submit. 'It's your fault you passed out.' The petty competition between us is at last doing its business and coming out into the open. My Opponent is tripping over her own feet. She sees me making him into an enemy. My first Enemy! I carry on preparing for my shower. I feel panicky.

'Fuck off!' he shouts, but he can't muster the volume. I note, with relief, that I've chosen a harmless enemy. It all fits, of course.

After all that was over with Tony I did some more thinking about Power.

Power is difficult. There is a set of rules that you need to know from the outset, otherwise it can get you into the nastiest sorts of trouble.

It's all right not to have it, and to be struggling to get it. Admirable, in almost any circumstances. The underdog, the lone man with a broken stride, is pitched against the entire fighting machine of the U.S. army. But when he finds the secret weapon, and suddenly he's got power on his side, woe betide him if he uses it. This is because something else comes along: Justice keeps on interfering with Power. It doesn't take over, it just tinkers with how nice Power is. The most admirable and honourable position is that of having absolute power but never using it. If you are going to use it, part of the deal is that you must have Justice on your side. So if the U.S. army has been cruel and malicious enough to the women and children our hero could fire the secret weapon and justifiably wipe out the entire land-force. That person fought for power and used it wisely. So the end of this argument is that when you've got power, it's OK to have it, as long as you don't use it against

200

the manners of Justice. The kung fu artist backs away from the whingeing octogenarian who's drunk and trying to goad him into a fight. The Soviet army lets the crippled dissident wheel himself to safety, away from the surrounded farmhouse. But, if you have power, and you use it without knowing your way round that difficult Justice ethic – well, if you do that you're disgusting.

Chrissy had power over me. It was because I was so much in trouble with physical cowardice. The sort of character she was, and her coming from the Screaming Maisonette, made it as though she was salting the wound, but of course she wasn't. She didn't know she had power over me, she certainly never used it, but she didn't need to. I took her power over me and rubbed myself up the wrong way with it; I used it against myself without her permission. Then I took the one little incident that gave me something to hit back with, and I clobbered her. It wasn't even a decent, strong sort of power that I used, it was a sneaky terrorist trick. I was only armed with a nanny and a handful of half-lies.

So, since this Tony incident that's how I've been looking at myself in relation to power. Poor Tony. He wasn't that bad, and now I've hurt him. There was the fearful thrill of having my first enemy, true. But even contained within the sporting ethos, as it was, the event made me ashamed. I don't want power, but I have to have more of it. It's the only thing that will get me out of this particularly disgusting predicament where I'm flailing around with what little potency I can find in myself and injuring myself, and Chrissy, and Tony . . . But I need to win a big enough wedge of power to get rid of my Opponent, to get to some place beyond her and the jigging, taunting dances of incitement that she does. I'm convinced that if I do manage to push past her to that place, it will be somewhere near where Toots is.

The approaching exam of Maria the waitress and her ex-boyfriend is going to be a marker in the measuring of my progress on this. Toots has set me up for something here. He's given me the opportunity, and he knows I'm afraid to need it. I think he's instinctively, cleverly, devious. There will be no sport about it, should it come. I will be needing physical bravery, the real thing, outside of the *dojo*. Won't the training just dissolve into something useless, what with all the fear? I can't predict what I'll do. This won't be a sporting fixture, but I crave the result for myself.

The flat survived my absence. The pictures looked a bit forgotten. They need to be looked at often, pictures, otherwise they go stale. If someone had kicked the door in, all they'd have got was a Hoover and some rudimentary furniture. It doesn't feel like home, now that the last of Chrissy's furniture has gone. What was the idea behind sending those removal men round without calling me first, or without them being able to tell me her new address? It wasn't meant as any sort of glancing blow to my pride; Chrissy doesn't use her power like that. There must be something else. Perhaps she has a jealous new boyfriend gnawing away at her past. I am part of her past . . . what a thought. I feel like moving somewhere else, right away out from amongst this constant atmosphere of loss.

The car is still working. Resigned to its own noises now.

February 20

You should have seen my ludicrous Opponent. She was ridiculously over-dressed for the occasion, wearing silk culottes

202

and a multi-coloured top hat, for God's sake! I was trussed tight with anxiety, but hypnotised by feeling the approach of a verdict. This is how it happened.

All four of us get into Toots' car. The work of Thursday night is finished; now we're into the early hours of Friday morning. Maria sits in the front after Nick and I have squeezed into the back. Toots drives very calmly. From my position behind him I like to watch the way his hands work the steering wheel: always both hands moving up to each other, never crossing over. The car turns smoothly, assisted by its own power. It smells of leather and Toots' perfume.

I am worried by the amount of material Toots holds on me. He unconsciously invites me to confide in him. Consequently he grows in stature. Tonight he is dangerously big. I feel like I'm seconding myself to his will-power in order to get to that place that's somewhere near him. I have to hold on hard to prevent myself feeling lost.

I remember Boiler's words. When I had asked Toots why he thought I was a racist pig he had shrugged it off: 'Nine out of ten white males in this country hate blacks,' he'd said, sitting like a king in his flat. 'What makes you think you're special?'

I like Maria. She is one of the only waitresses who has any inclination to spare me more than a few words for myself. She thinks I'm a spic too, probably. She wants to be friends. For the last week she's been apologising for 'causing such a fuss'. At the same time she is rather proud of Toots' attention. She was chattering wildly all tonight. I can't do that now the kitchen's getting busier. I didn't hear half of what she said.

The Boiler and José are walking home together. They give a wave as we drive past. Why did José come back? Toots' control seems magical sometimes.

Maria is talking about Roger: 'We tried, Jane and I, once, to get him to piss off. When he came in he saw Jane and asked me if I was a lesbian. I think he wanted me to be a lesbian. That would have let him off the hook. He sat down and started talking, droning on until our heads, you know, were dropping off our shoulders. Jane listened for, what, an hour? while I went and sat in the bog with Chéri and a good book. When I went back in he was crying like a baby. Jane had him in a bit of a comfort hug, telling him he had to leave me alone and whatever. I told him to piss off. It's only alcohol, see? If I'd been by myself he wouldn't have started all that crying. He can turn violent as quick as that!' Maria snaps her fingers and falls silent.

'Who's Chéri?' I ask.

'What?'

'You said you went and hid in the bog with someone called Chéri . . .'

'Oh yes, that's my snake. I have a snake called Chéri. She's often in the bathroom.'

'Oh. I see.' They get so trendy, these nightclub people.

Is this a brave mission? Have we got Justice on our side? I feel scared hearing about this pathetic insecure alcoholic, but the car is warm and full of people. It's a car with a gang in it, rolling along on expensive tyres that grip like hot slicks. The coloured code of road signs and traffic lights moves through the window like a video game. Toots' posh car is a white automatic box prowling through the fitted streets. This is a fairground ride that's going too fast, too high for me.

The alcoholic is sitting alone by the side of the road waiting for Maria to come back.

'That's Roger, there.'

Maria points at a dull red Cortina canted over in the gutter on the other side of the street. There he is. Toots speaks for the first time since getting in the car:

'Won't he go away when he sees us?'

'He's always come in before, whatever. He doesn't care.'

Maria leads the way across the road, ignoring the figure in the red Cortina. I say:

'He looks like a bag of potatoes.'

The nervous words don't seem to reach anyone else after leaving me. Toots moves across the road, his chest shaking gently as each heel hits the ground. I follow him. Where's Nick? I turn to see him leaning against the car, lighting a stick.

'Aren't you coming?'

'What d'you think, the car's more important, or no?'

I see his teeth flash in the darkness. He's a regular gang member. I'm the novice. I feel an uncomfortable gap between myself and my jacket. If I can one day fill this jacket with an increase in sinew and nerve . . .

Ahead of me Toots sinks down the steps to the basement flat. Maria is unlocking the door.

Inside the flat Toots is offered the best armchair. He accepts it as a matter of course. He says:

'Nice place, nice place.'

He's given no more than half a glance round the room. We're all automatic men with different switches. Maria asks me.

'Shall I take your coat?'

'No, it's all right thanks.'

She moves off to make coffee. Toots has produced his wallet and starts setting out the gear.

The Opponent, that malevolent old crone, has taken a front-row seat. She looks like she needs to visit the toilet because her knees are wobbling with excitement, knocking together to make a faint, insistent sound, nylon rubbing against nylon. Her fierce stare is fixed on me at all times, checking the strings across my chest and the leaks under my arms, assessing the content of my expression. It pleases her to know that every one of my bodily orifices feels on the point of opening suddenly to release the fear; there would be gushes and spurts, and her laughing.

When Maria reappears she shows me some of the damage her ex-boyfriend has caused. I tour around the flat behind her. The window is boarded-up in the middle sections. The door jamb is stuck together with glue and six-inch nails. She picks over a pile of cloth in the corner. She says:

'I've kept all this in case I need the evidence. He knew which were my favourites. Look! Cut to ribbons! He must have had a sharp knife.'

I think, 'Stanley Item. Not too dangerous for a stab. Only an inch deep. But if it crosses an artery? The neck . . . the wrist . . . the inner thigh . . . I have nothing to wrap round my wrists. Perhaps the coat is enough . . .' I run through the procedure for a knife coming in on an overarm strike. The block and then the outward twist that'll pull his elbow apart. If he does an underarm thrust or a straight jab it will be more difficult. I flex my ankles, thinking about the sideways avoidance.

Toots is sitting unconcerned with the stick burning between his fingers. The coffee stands untended on the tray beside him while he lifts his smoking arm back and forth to his mouth. I don't trust myself to make a try for the coffee graceful enough.

When the knock on the door breaks the waiting it's Maria who moves. She walks with a sulky face and opens the door, turning away immediately she has released the catch. She's not interested in looking at him. I hear a polite 'Hell – oh!' The alcoholic Roger sounds like a postman or a health visitor. When he comes into the room I see that he's scruffy and dressed in black. I think, 'It's a deception. Don't be fooled. Just because he looks friendly. Stay relaxed! Breathe!'

The sloping stranger ignores Toots and myself. He addresses himself only to Maria:

'I thought I'd drop in to say . . .'

'Bullshit!!' screams Maria. She's gone suddenly from the politeness of the drive and the coffee. She's been pushed into the open by him. I remember that this is the same nightmare for her every night. He persists in ignoring us. Toots is watching carefully, ready to get out of his chair.

'Give me a moment. I want to explain. You owe it to me to listen.' He smiles at her condescendingly. Although he is grovelling piteously, he's managed this grotesque show of pride and superiority, mocked up for the battle to show himself as decent.

'Roger . . . I have said a thousand fucking million times I don't want to see you or listen to you, ever!' Maria is going weak with fury and embarrassment. Toots stands up. Roger takes no notice, and starts to stalk slowly round the furniture in the direction of Maria's retreat. He says:

'There's several things you've got to own up to . . . things you haven't realised about yourself.'

'Fuck off!'

Toots steps forward and takes Roger by the arm. Roger takes no notice. Toots swings him round to sit him down in the armchair which he has just vacated. Roger is like a child in Toots' hands. Toots leans over him.

'Roger, can you hear me?'

'How d'you do?'

Roger holds out his hand. Toots ignores it.

'Roger, I want to say something. Afterwards you will leave. Then we will leave. If you return, we will return and hurt you. D'you understand?'

Roger is trying to throw his words round the side of Toots, to reach Maria:

'I'm not drunk.'

Maria has retired to a corner of the room, where she sits on a miniature hand-made wooden chair. She has put her forehead down to rest in her hands. Toots starts to give his message, tilting his face down closer to prevent Roger from looking at her.

'We are here to protect Maria against you. She isn't paying us. We are protecting her because she is our friend. You are hurting our friend. If you continue, we will hurt you.'

Roger has listened to this. He is blinking at Toots, whose face is only a breath's distance away from his own. Roger says, quietly:

'Boo.'

Toots is not offended. He stands upright and takes a step back, looking at Roger, speculating on the state of the man in front of him. Roger has now reverted to looking at Maria again. When Toots speaks he sounds more kindly.

'Now you leave. After that it's up to you.'

Roger gets up from the chair and goes to the front door. He turns conversational.

'It's a fine night.'

The three of us in the room are waiting for him to go. Roger himself has stopped with his hand on the door-catch, playing on our attention. He says:

'It's the sort of night which makes it great fun to go out and beat somebody up.' He leans backwards, saved from falling by holding onto the doorcatch.

'I think I'll go home and try and forget about myself.' He's swinging from side to side, still holding on.

'It's difficult. I might have to scrub myself . . .' He twists the latch and falls backwards. The door bangs against his feet and breaks his hold so he's on the floor. The door stands half open, reverberating from the knock. Laboriously he picks himself up. Toots and I are watching him. Maria is still hiding her face, sunk in anger and shame. Roger does nothing more but walk to the door and disappear from sight. His footsteps sound ordinary as he climbs the steps outside the boarded-up window.

Toots comes and stands in front of me. He looks blank and uninterested. His wallet is in his hand.

'You mind staying the night?'

'No, no, that's OK.'

Toots turns round to face Maria. The whole mass of his body turns at exactly the same time as his head. He decides to make the walk to the other side of the room. His voice is pitched low to Maria. I can't make it out, it's just the murmur of soothing words.

'. . . if that's all right with you.'

She nods her head. She's still angry. She doesn't attempt any return to the polite social bit. Toots retraces his steps to stand in front of me.

'If he comes back give him a slap and throw him out, mm?'

'OK.'

Toots touches me briefly on the shoulder of my coat. I wish my own shoulder had been there. Toots slips his wallet into his robe and treads a heavy path to the door. He doesn't look back before going out. This was just a delay. He's been on his way home all this time.

Maria has reached up to get the sleeping-bag from on top of the wardrobe. She lays it out on the sofa, and struggles briefly with the zip. She gets the pillow from her own bed. She's tired out and preoccupied with the year-long weight of this Roger problem, so we don't break in on each other. She thanks me for staying and shows me the bathroom. I choose not to spend too long in the bathroom, looking round carefully, not wanting to be surprised by the snake Chéri, who has remained invisible through all this. When I return Maria's in bed, either asleep or telling me she's asleep.

I make an assessment of the room. He could only get in by way of the door or the window. Either way I will wake up because he can't do it quietly. If he comes straight for me in the dark . . . I walk around the furniture, noting its position. I can put the sofa in between us. If he starts to climb over it, I can move behind the table. The light switch is by the doorway. There's a lamp behind me, which is the only source at the moment. Weapons? I let my eyes rest on objects. The lamp? No, it's clumsy because of the shade and the cord. A bottle rack has a few necks protruding. Quietly I go and take them out to hide them in various positions round the room.

A small black-handled Item is perched in the fruit bowl. I pick it out and grip the handle. It feels secure. There is a curve of plastic designed to prevent my hand from running onto the blade. I walk back with it to the sofa, and place it on the floor just by the castor. When I wake up, I run my hand down that corner and I'll find it immediately.

I move the lamp so I can control it from where I will be lying. The shadows are thrown higher now the lamp is on the floor. I can feel the light burning into my own face. I turn and look at my own shadow. It's halfway across the ceiling, big and reassuringly sinister. I take my jacket off, and my shirt, and insert myself into the sleeping-bag. I can use the shirt to wrap around my left wrist. There is nothing to protect my neck. It's a shame but I can't let myself wear my jacket in bed.

The Stanley knife comes at me from several different directions. Each time I have to think of a counteraction that can lead me into making my own attack. It's not enough to avoid the slash across the face; I must avoid, and having avoided, be in a position to retaliate with maximum force. The force will come from the ground and travel upwards, gathering additional strength from each part of the body. The horizontal swipe from the Stanley requires me to duck below it, but to duck forward, not backwards. I'll drop into an effective stance, really low, and take the man's ankles. The weight of his arm swinging across will help me to drive him sideways and lift his legs. He'll crash onto the back of his head. I'll have control of his legs. His genitalia will be wide open.

My Opponent shows no sign of fatigue. Her diseased eyes are glittering like an old dog's, and she's permanently ready to clap, or hiss. With Toots leaving me here like this, the occasion must have grown big enough for her. This must be all she will put me up for.

If the knife comes as a jab, I turn sideways. I mustn't go backwards. I turn and dab the force of his aim to one side, using both my hands, very light and fast: one, two. My fist

211

comes round into his temple. Three. In hard to the temple. Follow up with an arm-lock. Never lose the knife arm. Break the knife arm. Follow the knife and kill it. The little finger breaks as easy as a twig. The pain is important. The hand will be useless.

I won't sleep. Even with the light off and a conscious effort to control my breathing I don't even begin to approach the land of Nod. My ears are forced twice as hollow from straining to interpret the sounds of this creaking old building.

If only I could wear my jacket in bed. In the darkness I lie like an owl cast on its back.

I'm not venturing into sleep because it's too dangerous. Instead I find myself in difficulties on the boundaries of sleep. The boundaries are vaguely moving, cheating back and forth to trap me. The thoughts of the conscious mind are in danger of being taken and treated to a sinister process whereby the strange inventions of the subconscious take hold and run for a while before having to leave off. The unmistakable realism makes me sweat in the sleeping-bag.

I am on my way to visit Toots in his flat. I remember his rooms, all in cream and white, and as I walk I imagine him rolling about the place like a giant punctuation mark. Boiler will be downstairs, brooding in his own room which I've never seen into. He never fails to come upstairs at some point when I'm there. When he opens the door he will treat me blankly, not with open suspicion, and then turn away to return to his private skulking.

Toots' head is a giant dot on the top right-hand corner of the white six-seater settee. I hear his blank words again: 'I bought it from the foyer of some hotel.' There's the meandering melancholy of a blues man's voice, nearly singing; very skilful. It reminds me of death, and

212

Chrissy. She's had a death of her own. I'm isolated from it, here in these white rooms with the silver in Toots' teeth glinting. He's the stylist, there's no doubt, of his own life.

Toots has a pipe going. He lifts it from his mouth to point it at me and says:

'You hate blacks.'

'I don't. I know I don't.'

Toots points the pipe again, holding it right out in front of him as though he might be offering it to me.

'You,' he warns me, 'might one day get the same blood running through your head as runs through your heart.'

The pipe wavers over my body. Am I meant to take it? I continue to disclaim:

'I know that's not true. I just had the one thing happen that time . . .'

It's not the pipe that's waving at me. It's Toots' arm. He's holding his hand out to one side. When he has my attention he says:

'Here . . . look at this . . .'

He turns the palm of his hand so that it shows towards me.

'Which side d'you like best?'

He turns the hand back and forth. The pink palm ingrained with lines swaps with the black.

'Tell me when to stop,' says Toots, and then I can look at his silver teeth for a long time. This is unusual; I've always wanted to examine the teeth.

It's because Toots is laughing. We're standing by the car. I've not seen it happen before, and it chokes me that I can't join in.

After a long time of darkness Toots is back again in my view. I feel ghoulish, looking at his face so close up. The light reflects off his skin like it's a wet roof. There's a brown stain in the whites of his eyes. His mouth moves:

213

'Four out of five white men in this country hate the blacks.'

I reply, 'That's not true. Where did you get that?'

I feel my righteousness threatened. That is why I sound like I know what I'm talking about. Toots is confident:

'I got that from myself.'

'I just was frightened.'

'One man frightened you. So you blame his skin?'

'Not blame, fear . . .'

'Bullshit.'

It's good to have Toots' face so close. I search over the details of it. I feel greedy as well as hurt. The mouth in front of me moves like a machine to produce words:

'You watch out, now. I don't want you getting like those sort that are all in fashion, the whites that have the black friend that they do the handshake with, the ones that make up rules – how you not allowed to laugh at blacks unless they invite you to; how you got to be ten times more a friend to them than to anyone else. This is the worst guilty bullshit. In the next breath they say, these people, that they're the ones treating us right. They treat us like pets. Don't you get into one of these grey brains.'

Toots is going to take over. He's enormous and he has a plan. I need to form a system for retreating.

'You stay as one of the plain, ordinary guilty. They're the ones I like. You stay wrapping yourself up so as you can look up your own arse.'

'What d'you want?'

I must find out, although I already know. I'm still looking for a retreat. His face is looming.

'What d'you want?' I ask.

'I'm the one that hates the whites.'

'All of them?'

'All.'

'What d'you want?'

Toots is pulling at Boiler's hips. He doesn't appear to care about what he's doing.

'I've won,' he says, 'haven't I? I can have some fun with it now.'

The darkness of his face is slipping away, down into the colours of his robes. I must find out before it goes:

'What do I do? Tell me what to do!!'

Instead he talks to Boiler privately. I can't see anything. Is my head bowed in shame? Boiler leaves the room at a trot.

Toots' thighs are acres of space apart. When he laughs it jogs his belly.

'You say the words.'

'What words?'

'Only a couple of words.'

'I'll say them.'

Toots is holding himself open. He's laughing at me. There's the real pleasure of the laugh. I can hear it, but I can't see his face.

'OK,' he says laughing all the while, 'OK, say the words "I hate the blacks". Say them to yourself louder and louder in your own head and then say them to me.'

I have said the words to myself twice before I approach Toots, who's waiting on his sofa. I can just see the first of his chins stopping the robe from dropping back.

'Louder, I can't hear!' he says. I begin to mutter the words under my breath.

'Louder!' he repeats with the same laugh. I say firmly:

'I hate blacks.'

Toots' laughter takes off again. I must look stupid with my trousers *round my ankles. I know that his eyes will be uninterested. He's enormous and I'm advancing.*

'No wait!' he says. I stop. 'Wait . . . Stop right there.'

While I wait he gathers his breath and shouts at the top of his voice, 'Boiler! Boiler!!' We wait together, listening to the muffled slam of Boiler downstairs closing his door, and climbing the steps towards us. He's in the room. I can hear him behind me, although I don't turn round to look. Toots says:

'Before I deal with you I want you to go and stand in the corner. Over there.'

Boiler walks into my field of view and I see him wearing a leather jacket and a pair of silver silk briefs.

'Stand with your back to us.'

Boiler obeys, moving silently over the white carpet. He is standing where José was standing.

'We need to have the sound of someone crying in the background.'

There's a pause. Boiler seems to be gathering himself in the corner.

'Go on,' orders Toots, 'something miserable.'

Boiler starts to whine very softly, sounding like a puppy stuck indoors. Toots turns to look at me. I love him too much not to walk forward.

When I am brought to my senses by the sound of the door breaking I'm out of my bed in seconds with the entire bedside lamp in my hand. The switch does nothing. I must have broken it when I grabbed. The fear is virulent, burning a course through every nerve and making my jaw shake.

Roger switches the light on from the doorway. Maria gives a scream of last-ditch annoyance and dives under the bed-clothes, lying completely still. Roger speaks to me, fearlessly walking forwards round the furniture:

216

'There was a girl called Maria, who had the most beautiful rear . . .'

He starts to take his coat off, but then thinks differently about it. He puts one hand into a pocket, and keeps coming.

'She'd put it out . . .' he says, looking at me steadily, 'for any lout . . . who bought her a half-pint of beer . . .'

'Roger . . . what's the problem?' I sound like a bank manager, trying to officiate. Roger is standing by the corner of the settee, looking down at the sleeping-bag which lies there like an empty snake skin.

'The *problem*?' he asks, aghast that anyone can not know. 'The problem is . . . ' He's concentrating, looking fiercely inwards. 'Dear Marge,' he continues, frowning at me, 'I have a problem.' Now he looks at the ceiling, exposing his throat. 'Help . . . ! Help . . . !'

'Why are you doing this?' I plead with him. 'Why? Where can it possibly get you?'

'Nowhere,' he replies. 'Worse than nowhere. Some other place, worse than that. That's where it gets me.'

'So why not stop?'

He looks at me for some time with a friendly open face; then he sits on the sofa, but only momentarily, continuing the downward slide to the floor.

'God, I don't know,' he says, 'If I did know . . . what good is knowing? That wouldn't stop me. I do it, because I do it, because I do it . . .'

'You could stop doing it,' I reply, helpfully, almost jocular. 'There is that possibility. It is a possible choice, to stop doing anything.'

'Not this. I've put the brakes on everything else. Work.

217

Family. Friends. Eating. I'm good at stopping things. But this is running away with me.'

Maria is still motionless under the bedclothes at this stage. I can't even see her breathing, but she must be listening to us.

I ask, 'How did it all start?'

'I just want to be treated with some respect. That's all it was, anyway, from the beginning. Now ... she *owes* me something. I don't know what it is, but when we finished, when she finished with me, she kept something that was mine.'

'I know the feeling.'

'Whatever it is, she's got to understand, she's got to give it back. She *owes* it to me.'

'I don't think she can give it back. You've got to find it somewhere else, haven't you?' I listen with amazement to my own rational advice. Maybe I ought not to be giving it; maybe I ought to be keeping this advice for myself.

'But it's here,' says Roger savagely, 'I know it is. In this room, I lost it ... She's got it!' he exclaims, pointing at the hump of bedclothes. Tears are melting his expression.

'She hasn't,' I say, earnestly, repeating the words again for pity's sake.

'God, I'm so tired,' he says, crying openly, the phrases staggered on long shaky breaks, 'I'm ...' He looks at me in surprise, 'I really am ... exhausted.'

'So is she.'

Roger nods, dumbly, squandering tears. After a long while, and I mean long, maybe after ten minutes of us just sitting and Maria maintaining her motionless evasion, Roger gets to his feet and goes to the bathroom. When the sound of the rushing water has finished he reappears, with one end of a dressing-gown cord wrapped round his neck, the other end being held

218

aloft by his upstretched arm. His arm tugs upwards, and his neck snaps sideways comically. The dressing-gown cord is twisting in his hand.

'There was a young man called Roger,' he says, with difficulty, 'who always wanted to knob 'er. He broke down the door, with a drunken roar, but utterly failed to dislodge 'er.'

So his performance ends there with a last tug and a grimace. When he breaks his position I see it is not a dressing-gown cord, but the snake, Chéri, who's now coiling angrily in his hands as he walks towards me. She must be harmless, but snakes never look harmless. They always look as though they're determined to be as violently poisonous as possible, and high-status to boot.

'She gets angry if she's put in here,' says Roger, letting the creature eel out from amongst his arms. 'She only likes it in the bathroom.'

The snake disappears under the furniture. It must be satisfying, to move like that, sinuous and well lubricated.

'D'you know,' I say to Roger, 'I was meant to hit you and throw you out if you came back.'

'I know,' he says.

'I'm glad I didn't.'

'So am I,' he replies, with ridiculous exaggeration. We both start laughing. 'Get out!' he cries at me, shaking a rolled-up fist, 'get out or I'll hit you!' Towards the end of our laugh, which carries on, stupidly gutteral and perpetuating itself from one open mouth to the other, I see the bedclothes move and Maria makes a slight sound. It's impossible to tell whether she's annoyed or joining in. Roger doesn't notice, because this is when he's taking the gun from his pocket and laying it on

219

the floor beside him. A gun; a drill; a hole-punch; a hammerer of human plumbing; automatic Death.

March 13

As for what's happening right now, it amounts to nothing but a pile of bags and a man in a room moving through the middle of a March night, not tired at all. It's tea-time for me.

I managed to find some of that plastic bubbly stuff in a skip, which I've used to wrap my pictures; they're leaning against the wall, their constant message muffled in what looks like space-costumes. The bags are in the middle of the lounge here; a big canvas one, the white judo bag, and a bin-liner full of clothes. There's more to do in the kitchen yet, but I prefer to be here doing this. I feel wrong, clanking about when there's such orangey dark quietness outside. Hundreds of people are sleeping all around me. I could probably put my hand through the paper-thin wall and steal someone's sleep if I wanted to. Instead I'll carry on for a bit, before starting on the kitchen. After all, I have some important news.

I'm hiding in the bus queue. Persistent rain is dragging the smog particles down out of the sky. The roads shine and hiss with traffic. The bus queue is impatient under the rattling little shelter, but I'm not waiting for the bus, I'm following Chrissy. My hands stick in my soggy pockets as I try to find as much loose change as I can. I've no idea where I'm going, how much I'll need. I reorganise my scarf to hide the bottom half of my face, and curse the water escaping down my collar. Where will I sit on the bus?

Chrissy is first in the queue and I see her clearly step up onto the platform and take the stairs to the top deck. She's wearing a red plastic mac, which makes her easy to follow. One by one we press onto the bus. The ideal place for me to sit would be on one of the long sideways seats at the back, where I'd have a clear view of the stairs. Unfortunately they're all taken, mostly by old people with wet nylon clothes and shopping bags between their ankles. In my forward-facing seat, I'll have to turn round every time the bus comes to a halt. I don't even know what number this bus is.

It's quite a slow journey through heavy traffic. Everyone else seems to know exactly where they're going. They are all impatient little animals striving to get home to have food. We're all chasing our lives through the rain. A fat lady who has been running sits steaming in front of me.

Chrissy might not be going home. She might be heading out to some friend's place. When I look out of the window I can't recognise anything. The bus trundles on through the gears.

I have to ask for a 50 pee fare and hope that the conductor doesn't notice if I stay on for longer than that. I hand the money over, realising that I don't have any cash left to get back. If it comes down to it I can call a cab to get to work and scrounge some money there. It won't matter if I'm late. Boiler can start preparing. The conductor is winding my individual snippet of bog-paper from out of the machine round his neck. Once the paper is in my hand I see the red mac standing on the rear platform. The bus is stopped at a traffic light, and Chrissy carefully gets off. I rise, meeting the conductor's back in the passageway. I try to push past. He's saying:

'Well, you know this isn't a fifty, this is a thirty . . .'

I push harder and pass him. When I get to the back of the

bus the road is moving beneath the platform. Nevertheless I step off. The road pulls me into an immediate run, and after my feet slap twice, heavily, on the wet road, I fall forward. God bless judo for the forward roll; I'm on my feet and unhurt. When I look round to find the red mac I'm aware of several people giving me the worried Shortest Possible Glance. Chrissy is staring at me. She's standing on the pavement with her mouth open. I walk up to her with the rising hysteria making me nippy and light-footed. I say:

'I'm sorry. I was following you.'

'Your hand's bleeding.'

I lift my hand, wishing that she had taken it and offered to do something. I see that the heel of it has been scraped down to release the blood. Her plastic coat makes a loud noise like a roof in the rain. My other hand is bleeding. What a mess. I ask:

'D'you live near by?'

'Not far.'

'Would you mind if I came in and got sorted out? I've got no money. I just saw you, and followed you. It was all on the spur of the moment.'

She is fiddling in her bag. Everything is urgent and slippery because of the rain. It's like we've got no time to be doing this. She's going to give me money. This is horrible. What am I, a nuisance? Is that all?

'Can I return sometime to pay you back?'

'I don't think it's worth it,' she mumbles kindly.

She has extracted a pound coin and holds it out for me to take. I am surprised by my own hand when I hold it out; because of the rain the blood has thinned and spread all over my fingers. It drips and gleams like a horror prop, complete

222

with black grit from the road. She puts the money back in her purse.

'It's not far,' she says. 'Come on.'

I follow obediently. Later I dare to catch up and walk alongside her. Like all the other pedestrians, we are bent by the rain.

The house is a tiny terraced two-up two-down, with a small garden at the front. We go in without saying a word. She's in a hurry to get rid of me.

Chrissy takes me upstairs and puts some Dettol in a basin full of warm water for my hands. I admire her haircut.

'It's not new. I've had it like this for ages.'

'New for me, then.'

I hate this type of thing. This isn't what I wanted, this effort at dragging the old time to meet the new time, which makes you aware of nothing so much as trudging over the gap in between. I can only stumble on.

She's not talking very much, but her patting of my hands with the towel is considerate.

Downstairs in the kitchen she is making us tea. She stands by the kettle, waiting, marking the floor with her foot.

'I'm sorry about whoever it was who died.'

'What?'

'Tony told me. About the house, and whatever. I hope it was nothing terrible.'

'Oh yes. Tony.'

'Still, it's a lovely place.'

'Yes. It's a blessing.'

'D'you see Tony much?'

'Only once in a while. Do you?'

'Not much any more.'

She's not drinking her tea. It stands there steaming. Perhaps I'm steaming, like the old lady on the bus. I'm chasing so *hard*. I'm going to carry on despite her reluctance. I want to move on to something difficult.

'Umm, I had nothing in mind when I followed you. I mean I saw you, and I wanted to speak to you, but I didn't have the courage, so of course while I was failing to have the courage I ended up following you.'

'I see.'

'Are you doing anything? I don't want to hold you up.'

'I do have to get ready in a while. But not for a bit.'

The kitchen is cheaply put together from bits of junk furniture. It feels like a useful, busy room. I ask:

'D'you live here alone?'

'Yes,' she replies, defending herself, from me moving in maybe.

'I'm surprised you can manage.'

She stirs uncomfortably against the plastic laminate surface.

'I did think of having a lodger.'

'You could charge a fortune.'

'I didn't want anyone else here.'

I imitate the film star: 'I want to be alone.'

'Yes, that's just what I do want, as it happens.'

'So quite solitary these days, then?'

'Yes.'

My hands are throbbing under the cotton wool pads.

'All right. I'll go soon.'

'No, I didn't mean that . . . I meant . . .'

I watch as she tries to go on. I am trying to think of a way of finding out why she never got in touch with me after my reply. That is where our relationship left off, and we need to go back

224

to that point in order to carry on. She owes me something, as Roger would say.

My courage is stoppered up enough to prevent me from talking. Instead tears flow. A wretched substitute. She's embarrassed for me as I try to excuse myself.

'I'm sorry . . . I don't know what . . . perhaps I ought to go.'

'Don't be silly. Stay for a bit longer. Let me take your coat and put it to dry.'

'No, it's all right, I'll keep it on . . .'

'Give it over!'

She takes the soaked cloth and disappears while I recover. I'm looking out of the kitchen window across a small yard. There's someone else's kitchen window, with curtains across it. In that kitchen there's somebody sitting . . . and beyond that kitchen there's another kitchen . . . and all of us are thinking that we're in the exact middle of the universe. There is no finite measure of possible sadness. My hands are sad. They're in a sad state.

When she comes back to the table and sits down to talk to me I remind myself that I might have been crafty here. She says:

'I'm sorry I never wrote back.'

'I thought it was you who was so keen to get things sorted out.'

'I was. But I changed my mind.'

'Why?'

'I can't say. I just did. I thought that nothing much could help us so I might as well not carry on talking.'

We stop talking there, for obvious reasons. I drink my tea. The cotton wool on my hands is as white as the powder in Toots' wallet. Had I been crafty, holding out my hands like

that, straight out in front of her? How many of the tears were
just a demand for a longer tea break? I ask:

'What did you think of my reply?'

'It frightened me, actually.'

'Why?'

'Well . . . it was so long. It was really very long, and it was all
. . . It was all *you*. And it was frightening.'

'I see. Did it explain anything, at all?'

'Yes. I felt sorry for you. But there was no answer I could
give. It was still you . . . living from day to day; just you.'

'But that's exactly what you asked for! What was I meant to
do? Write about my mother?'

'We can't talk now.'

'Why not?'

'We just can't. Look, come back another time.'

'I want . . . I need to sort it out . . .'

In fact I don't need, I don't even want, to sort anything out.
All I want is to touch her. She's looking pale.

'We will sort it out. But later.'

'Why not now?'

'Please, can we leave it? And look . . . Wednesday. What
about Wednesday? I'll meet you in town.'

'I work at night.'

'What about the daytime on Saturday?'

'Umm . . .'

'Phone me. It's impossible now. I can't concentrate. I'm
meant to be going out. Please go.'

'All right.'

'I'm sorry. You must go. I'll get your coat.'

She looks frightened. When we are both in the hall and I'm
putting my hands into the coat she's holding out, I ask her:

'Where are you going?'

'Just round to a friend's.'

'I'm after a lift.'

'Oh, no, I'm walking.'

'Ah, I need your telephone number. Pen and paper?'

She trots up the stairs willingly enough. I'm not forcing the number out of her. She reappears and writes the number very large with her name. It's a bad sign that she includes her surname. She's holding the door open for me. Has she forgotten? I'll have to ask:

'Could I, d'you think, borrow that bit of money? I just jumped on the bus, you see . . .'

She's already gone. She smiled before turning back indoors. I have a gloomy thought: 'She's being friendly because I'm about to go.'

Finally, when I have my pound coin and we've done the goodbye, I say:

'You know, it is true, what I said in the reply. And I'm sorry. I apologise. I think it's all gone now anyway.'

'Give me a call,' she replies, closing the door while waving at the same time. It's stopped raining, at least.

I am no more than a few yards down the road when I stop walking. Something has risen like a trout to surprise me. I realise that I'm looking at Mr Popupandseeme. The sight of him is a kickback, a mystery, a series of immediate questions. I stand stopped in my tracks, dead still. An extraordinary sight! He won't see me unless he turns round to look over his shoulder. He is sitting in his car parked over on the other side of the road. There he is. I mouth the name quietly to myself.

A massed jumble of things are suddenly remembered. Mr Popupandseeme! He is reading a newspaper laid out on the steering wheel of his car. He is slumped in a big coat with a flap of collar turned up on the back of his neck. The car is a red Mercedes, newly shined. The rain stands in bubbles all over the surface of it.

He picks up a page. It looks like a tabloid newspaper, open at the racing section. He lets the page drop and runs his hand through his hair, arranging the flops across his crown in a practised shift of his hand. The top of his head is not flattered by the interior light. As his wrist drops again, he checks the watch.

Soon he will visit Chrissy. He doesn't want to be early. She's been strict with him. She's told him to come at a particular time, and he obeys, right on the very point of her command. I would guess that he always pulls up early, and waits, to be sure of never being late and missing precious seconds of his allotted time with her.

Grand conclusions jump at me while I stand there holding my luck. The house?

I am flabbergasted.

At whatever moment he cares to open the car door and get out I'm ready to turn tail and walk the other way. For now I stand and watch his innocent reading.

I am responsible for this. I shoved Chrissy up against the belly of this fat obvious man. She'd have the weight of that stomach rolling on top of her. He would try to hang it up on his stubby arms, his bunched fists sunk into the mattress each side of her, but to no avail. There wouldn't be one position in the *Kama Sutra* which could get you away from that belly. Perhaps it's erotic, like a single giant rolling hairy breast with

228

an inverted nipple. She gets to go to her very own bathroom afterwards, of course.

I cast around for a place to hide. I could watch him calling on her, and see her reaction to him. The Greeting Kiss.

I've seen enough. It would be horrible for her if anything went wrong. I have her phone number in my pocket. I turn back the opposite way, leaving Mr Popupandseeme oblivious in his red Mercedes. Does he know he was called Mr Popup-andseeme? Perhaps they have pet names. He calls her Christina, or Sweetheart. She would call him Gut Bucket.

My feet are still soaking wet. They're rubbing sore in my shoes as I try to find my way back to the bus by another route. The light has failed miserably. Even now Mr Popupandseeme will be handing over the chocolates and the flowers. Chrissy will have the hall light on. His grey face will break into a smile, and Chrissy will have to kiss the two greasy strips of lip. The thought of bacon will make me salivate, if I don't stop thinking of our joke about his lips.

It's a tragedy. It's beneath the gossip. It's bigger than the surprise. It's a sickening trap that's closed over a friend of mine. She's gone. I now tear the phone number in half and let it go. The slabs of cotton wool on my hands make it difficult, and the bits of paper flash in the descending gloom.

Straight home after that lot. A bit of pacing about. I change my clothes and hang around waiting to go to work. And then out loud I tell the flat, 'I don't want you any more.' By the time I get in my car, the traffic has scattered.

All this added up to swing the decision in favour of leaving the flat. I'm leaving for good. I know I'm right. Chrissy has

229

disappeared, suddenly she has gone, and there is a novelty angle: I don't want her any more.

It's been freezing tonight. Now in the first light you can see the cold the other side of the glass. It's taken things into its grip. They are shriven with cold.

I was in the same state when Roger had put the gun down on the floor next to him: I felt the brittle blueness of rigor mortis stealing over me. All conversation stopped. Roger stayed looking at the gun for some time, working it out. He murmured quietly, 'I'm glad you didn't . . .', saying the words for himself. What was the best thing to do in those circumstances? I tried to appear as though nothing had changed. I pretended to ignore the gun, make out we were still friends. At the same time I was working out how to deal with it. I kept on talking. There was no training in me for a gun . . . no moves, no deceptions, no hold-downs. There was no answer. I'd had it, hadn't I?

Armed! He'd come armed, and I'd have got my face wiped with egg all right. As I talked on and on, wishing that my voice could hold a steady tone, I thought about some policeman I'd read about, who had rammed his finger in behind the trigger of a gun he was struggling with, to prevent it from being fired. This was the only plan I had. The gun was lying there . . . How far away was his hand?

'It's all right', said Roger.

'What?'

'The pistol was only dangerous *before* I took it out of my pocket.'

I looked at him wearing his sad smile; I could hardly believe it. Was it all because it had turned out that we could speak?

230

Free to go now, and with a rush, the prickly fear dropped away, and, as part of the same zooming freedom, I saw that the appearance of the pistol on the carpet next to him also meant something else: I'd been successful. I felt a hysterical calmness, and a sense of wonder. I felt humbleness ... wonderful, invigorating humbleness; I was rich with it, as though I had found it for myself, won it, earned it. I felt the simple veracious charm of *humility*. But also, in this spell of rising excitement, I was conscious of its power. Humility had a magical power, an easy, incorruptible, enjoyable power ... I had been successful. With just a few words I had disarmed a raging armed lunatic.

Unaware of my emotion, Roger meanwhile had been tearing off a small scrap of paper. I couldn't see what was written on it. He rubbed it into a ball between his fingers and put it in his mouth to chew it.

'Anyway,' he said, 'don't know what makes you think that you were the target.'

I couldn't reply, because of being suddenly locked into waiting for what would be next. He lifted the pistol and pointed it at his own head, still chewing steadily. I didn't say a word, or move; looking back on it I think it must have been that I didn't want to make any difference, I wanted to it to be entirely dependent on his decision. He pulled the trigger, and there was a loud 'twang'. He hissed through his teeth, and put his hand up to where the gun had pointed, rubbing furiously and saying, 'OWW ... UCH' under his breath several times and rocking back and forth. He was laughing again, pressing the heel of his hand against his head. 'Ouch ...' he repeated, and laughed at the ceiling. It was an air-pistol.

He broke the gun in half, pushing with difficulty all the way back against the travel of the spring, took the chewed-up pellet of paper from his mouth and pushed it into the top of the barrel. Then he closed it and held it out to me. 'You have a go,' he said.

'No thanks. It looks very sore.'

'Hurts like shit!'

He stood up and trod lightly towards Maria's motionless form. He was searching round the edge of the bedding. Finding nothing, he began to insert the barrel very carefully underneath one corner.

'No. Roger . . .' I joined him and we struggled briefly for control of his wrist. Twang! The pellet flew somewhere harmless. Maria remained inert and unharmed.

Roger and I talked for about three hours that night. We ran back and forth across his relationship with Maria, and also mine with Chrissy. Roger shot himself four more times in various sensitive parts of his body. There came often a repeated phrase in our conversation, a key line, a laugh line, a refrain: 'I wish I could stop doing this.'

He left when it got to daylight, taking the pistol with him to return it to the person he'd borrowed it off. I lay down on the sofa, exhausted. Maria still showed no sign of movement. She told me that she did fall asleep, waking up every now and again, surprised to hear the voices still going on.

I remember Maria coming into the kitchen at work that time, a few days after it was all over. She was shouting; she always raised her voice when she was working hard. 'Eh, you!' she said, standing very close to me, 'I hate you, you know that . . .' She paused to put her finger under my nose, 'I hate you, you . . . you . . . what are you, I hate you . . . you *talker*! I know what you've gone and done.'

232

'What?' I asked, smiling.

'You ... have ... gone ...' she continues, talking with exaggerated, disbelieving annoyance, 'and got friendly with him. You have adopted Rog – errrr!'

'God, I'm sorry,' I replied.

'Sorry's not enough! I don't believe you, you talker, that's what you are!' She shook her head at me before going out of the swing door.

Boiler took the opportunity to get his own back. He still calls me Talker now, mocking my short-lived fame after the incident.

I have seen Roger several times since. We make agreements and carry out small-scale plans together. We have developed a pattern of behaviour to amuse ourselves, with him drinking still pretty hard. When we went to the Screaming Maisonette it was being squatted by an individual who had a pile of cardboard arranged as a bed in the corner. Roger gave him all the money he had; he emptied his pockets and pushed it through the letter box when the guy refused to open the door to us. I don't know whether he needed it, that's not the point; we were doing it to get to our favourite feeling, the one we amuse ourselves chasing, the feeling of release, escaping from the pressure.

We decided that when we move in, we'll take the locks off the door. That will be a major excitement, no locks. What will happen? I'm looking forward to it. I couldn't have done it alone.

It's working up towards morning out there, now. In here I'm nearly done with my day. The kitchen's packed, the two large boxes stacked by the door. Not that I'll need that sort of stuff, where I'm going. The only thing I'm leaving behind is the picture of The Old Woman Washing Up.

This woman, my mobile picture, is going through her normal pattern of movements, the first set of the day, and it's a relatively easy start, the breakfast things. You can make out the sudsy water running off the breakfast plates as she lifts them one by one onto the rack. She's wearing a green cardigan that fits like a sack. I would like to see her escape from her red-painted wooden square. Her arms look too capable of strength to be wasted on crockery. They've gone flabby and loose round the bone, soggy from washing-up water.

Staring at her window, but looking through mine, I am conscious that I might make a picture for somebody else. I've stood doing nothing for two and a half years, appearing at odd times of the day and night. It might feature as a picture entitled *Figure Waiting*. I have fooled myself that I've been on an internal journey. In fact I have been nowhere. I've just caught a glimpse of my own back.

I can see the little schoolboy dog-owner on his way to class. I imagine his middle drawer still sealed round the edges with skin. It'll be quiet in there at the moment. His Opponent is perfectly formed, but dormant, with the lids covering her eyes unbroken, ready for the day when the drawer falls open. There is an empty brown space in the Dali painting. Plenty of room. He'd fit in nicely.

My mad old witch-bitch, the useless gap-toothed bladder bag, is still there, chewing her fingers in the middle drawer. She has aged, there's no doubt. The differences are quite clear. She's lost moisture. You can tell she's drying out because there's a rattle now when she sucks her thumb. There's no

234

saliva in her mouth so the act of sucking makes her teeth rattle. She's in the middle drawer for ever, I think. She rarely comes out now. I can hear her dried-out knee joints creaking. She is always thinking; you know, the same old things, always the same old things. These thoughts have twisted her eyes out of skew, they are that repetitive, that constantly forceful. However, I think she is capable of death, she is up to that.

Time to take the well-worn path to bed. It's nine o'clock in the morning.

Current and forthcoming titles from Sceptre

CHRISTOPHER BURNS

ABOUT THE BODY

JONATHAN COE

A TOUCH OF LOVE

RONALD FRAME

PENELOPE'S HAT

RICHARD RUSSO

THE RISK POOL

PAUL SAYER

THE COMFORTS OF MADNESS

BOOKS OF DISTINCTION